Letters from
Father Christmas

By Elf Messenger

J.R.R. Tolkien
Letters from Father Christmas
Edited by Baillie Tolkien

TED SMART

This edition produced for The Book People Ltd,
Hall Wood Avenue, Haydock, St Helens WA11 9UL

HarperCollins*Publishers*
77–85 Fulham Palace Road,
Hammersmith, London W6 8JB

www.**fire**and**water**.com
www.tolkien.co.uk

This edition published by HarperCollins*Publishers* 1999
1 3 5 7 9 8 6 4 2

First published by George Allen & Unwin 1976

ISBN 0 007 66371 4

Set in Belwe Bold, Sanvito Light and Palatino
Design: Amzie Viladot Lorente

Origination by Saxon Photolitho

Printed and bound in Dubai, UAE

Introduction

To the children of J. R. R. Tolkien, the interest and importance of Father Christmas extended beyond his filling of their stockings on Christmas Eve; for he wrote a letter to them every year, in which he described in words and pictures his house, his friends, and the events, hilarious or alarming, at the North Pole. The first of the letters came in 1920, when John, the eldest, was three years old; and for over twenty years, through the childhoods of the three other children, Michael, Christopher and Priscilla, they continued to arrive each Christmas. Sometimes the envelopes, dusted with snow and bearing Polar postage stamps, were found in the house on the morning after his visit; sometimes the postman brought them; and the letters that the children wrote themselves vanished from the fireplace when no one was about.

As time went on, Father Christmas' household became larger, and whereas at first little is heard of anyone else except the North Polar Bear, later on there appear Snow-elves, Red Gnomes, Snow-men, Cave-bears, and the Polar Bear's nephews, Paksu and Valkotukka, who came on a visit and never went away. But the Polar Bear remained Father Christmas' chief assistant, and the chief cause of the disasters that led to muddles and deficiencies in the Christmas stockings; and sometimes he wrote on the letters his comments in angular capitals.

Eventually Father Christmas took on as his secretary an Elf named Ilbereth, and in the later letters Elves play an important part in the defence of Father Christmas' house and store-cellars against attacks by Goblins.

In this book it has been possible to give only a few examples of Father Christmas' shaky handwriting, but almost all the pictures that he sent are here reproduced; and also included is the alphabet that the Polar Bear devised from the Goblin drawings on the walls of the caves where he was lost, and the letter that he sent to the children written in it.

for Christmas

NORTH POLE —
22 DEC, 1920

2 kisses
NORTH POLE POSTAGE

OXFORD

Mrs Tolkien :—
—: & :—
Master John Francis Reuel Tolkien
1 Alfred Street
St Giles
Oxford
— England

1920

Dear John

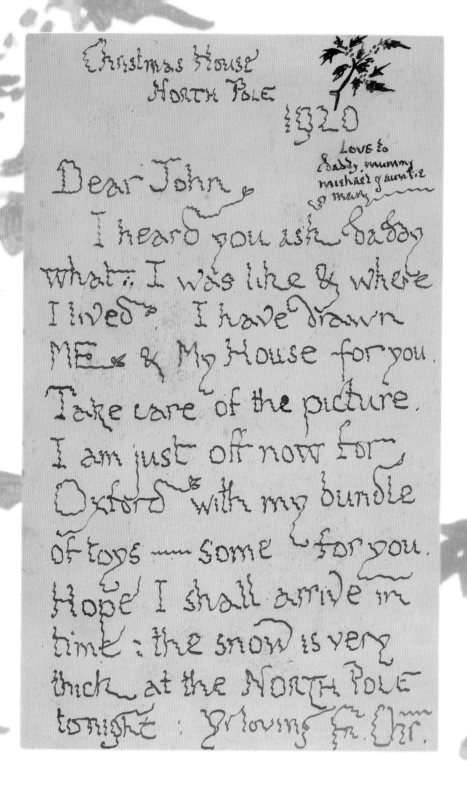

Christmas House, North Pole
22nd December 1920

Dear John

I heard you ask daddy what I was like and where I lived. I have drawn me and my house for you. Take care of the picture. I am just off now for Oxford with my bundle of toys – some for you. Hope I shall arrive in time: the snow is very thick at the North Pole tonight. Your loving Father Christmas

DEC. 23
1923

NORTH · POLE
POST

Master John Francis Tolkien
11. St Marks Terrace
Woodhouse Lane
Leeds

1923

Fr. Nicholas Christmas

North Pole
Christmas Eve: 1923

My dear John,

It is very cold today and my hand is very shaky – I am nineteen
hundred and twenty four, no! seven! years old on Christmas
Day, – lots older than your great-grandfather, so I can't stop the
pen wobbling, but I hear that you are getting so good at
reading that I expect you will be able to read my letter

Christmas Eve : 1923

North Pole

My dear John

It is very old to day and
my hand is very shaky ——
I am nineteen hundred and twenty
no! seven!
four years old on Christmas day,—
is older than your great-grandfather,
so I can't stop the pen wobbling.
but I hear that you are getting
so good at reading that I expect
you will be able to read my letter

13

on Christmas day,

I send you lots of love (and lots for Michael too) and Lotts
Bricks too (which are called that because there are lots more for
you to have next year if you let me know in good time). I think
they are prettier and stronger and tidier than Picabrix.
So I hope you will like them.

Now I must go; it is a lovely fine night and I have got hundreds
of miles to go before morning – there is such a lot to do.

A cold kiss from

Father Nicholas Christmas

lots of love

North Pole

I send you lots of love and lots for Michael too, and Lots Bricks too which are called that because there are lots more for you to have next year if you let me know in good time. I think they are prettier and stronger and tidier than Picabrix, so I hope you will like them. Now I must go; it is a lovely fine night and I have got hundreds of miles to go before morning — there is such a lot to do. & cold kisses from

Fr. Nicholas Christmas

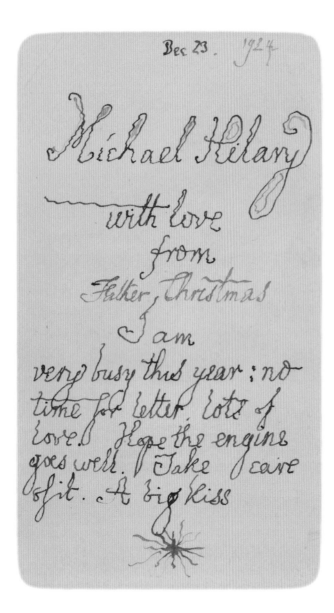

Dear Michael Hilary

I am very busy this year: No time for
letter. Lots of love. Hope the engine goes
well. Take care of it. A big kiss.

with love from
Father Christmas

December 23rd 1924

Dear John

Hope you have a happy Christmas. Only
time for a short letter, my sleigh is
waiting. Lots of new stockings to fill this
year. Hope you will like station and
things. A big kiss.

with love from
Father Christmas

£924

NP NP
X 2 4

NORTH 1924 POLE.

Master Michael Hilary Reuel Tolkien.
2 Darnley Road
West Park
Leeds

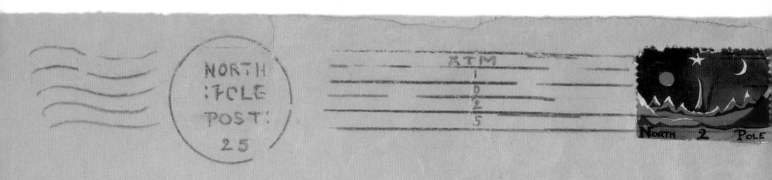

Masters John & Michael Tolkien
2 Darnley Road
West Park
LEEDS
England
Europe
the World ⋮

1925

Cliff House
Top of the world
near the North Pole

me

Cliff House, Top of the World, Near the North Pole
Christmas 1925

My dear boys,

I am dreadfully busy this year – it makes my hand more shaky than ever when I think of it – and not very rich; in fact awful things have been happening, and some of the presents have got spoilt, and I haven't got the North Polar bear to help me, and I have had to move house just before Christmas, so you can imagine what a state everything is in, and you will see why I have a new address, and why I can only write one letter between you both.

It all happened like this: one very windy day last November my hood blew off and went and stuck on the top of the North Pole. I told him not to, but the North Polar Bear climbed up to the thin top to get it down – and he did. The pole broke in the middle and fell on the roof of my house, and the North Polar Bear fell through the hole it made into the dining room with my hood over his nose, and all the snow fell off the roof into the house and melted and put out all the fires and ran down into the cellars, where I was collecting this year's presents, and the North Polar Bear's leg got broken.

He is well again now, but I was so cross with him that he says he won't try to help me again – I expect his temper is hurt, and will be mended by next Christmas.

I send you a picture of the accident and of my new house on the cliffs above the North Pole (with beautiful cellars in the cliffs). If John can't read my old shaky writing (one thousand nine hundred and twenty-five years old) he must get his father to. When is Michael going to learn to read, and write his own letters to me? Lots of love to you both and Christopher, whose name is rather like mine.

That's all: Good Bye
Father Christmas

P. S.

Father Christmas was in a great hurry – told me to put in one of his magic wishing crackers. As you pull, wish,

Cliff House
Top of the world
Near the North Pole

Xmas
1925

Xmas
1925

My dear boys

I am dreadfully busy this year — it makes my hand more shaky than ever when I think of it — and I'm not very rich: in fact awful things have been happening, and some of the pres-ents have got spoilt, and I haven't got the North Polar bear to help me, and I have had to move house just before Christmas, so you can imagine what a state everything is in, and you will see why I have a new address, and why I can write only one letter between you both. It all happened like this: one very windy day last November my hood blew off and went and stuck on the top of the North Pole. I told him not to, but the N.P. Bear climbed up to the thin top to get it down — and he did. The pole broke in the middle and fell on the roof of my house, and the N.P. Bear fell through the hole it made into the dining room with my hood over his nose, and all the snow fell off the roof into the house and melted and put out all the fires and ran down into the cellars where I was collecting this year's presents, and the N.P. Bear's leg got broken. He is well again now, but I was so cross with him that he says he won't try to help me again till next Christmas. I expect his temper is hurt, and will be mended by next Christmas. I send you a picture of the accident, and of my new house on the cliffs above the N.P. (with beautiful cellars in the cliffs). If John can't read my old shaky writing (1925 years old) he must get his father to. When is Michael going to learn to read, and write his own letters to me? Lots of love to you both and Christopher, whose name is rather like mine.

That's all. Goodbye. Father Christmas

P.S.

me

FR Christmas was in great hurry — told me to put in one of his magic wishing crackers. As you pull, wish, & see if it doesnt come true. Excuse thick writing I have a fat paw. I help Fr C. with his packing: I live with him. I am the

GREAT (Polar) BEAR

and see if it doesn't come true. Excuse thick writing I have a fat paw. I help Father Christmas with his packing: I live with him. I am the

GREAT (Polar) BEAR

John, Michael, & Christopher Tolkien.

22 Northmoor Road

Oxford

England

by Southern Post

A merry Christmas to you

Christmas 1926

And love from Father Christmas
to you all.

Cliff House, Top of the World, Near the North Pole
Monday December 20th 1926

My dear boys,

I am more shaky than usual this year. The North Polar Bear's fault! It was the biggest bang in the world, and the most monstrous firework there ever has been. It turned the North Pole BLACK and shook all the stars out of place, broke the moon into four – and the Man in it fell into my back garden. He ate quite a lot of my Christmas chocolates before he said he felt better and climbed back to mend it and get the stars tidy.

Then I found out that the reindeer had broken loose. They were running all over the country, breaking reins and ropes and tossing presents up in the air. They were all packed up to start, you see – yes it only happened this morning: it was a sleighload of chocolate things, which I always send to England early. I hope yours are not badly damaged.

But isn't the North Polar Bear silly? And he isn't a bit sorry! Of course he did it – you remember I had to move last year because of him? The tap for turning on the Rory Bory Aylis fireworks is still in the cellar of my old house. The North Polar Bear knew he must never, never touch it. I only let it off on special days like Christmas. He says he thought it was cut off since we moved.

Anyway, he was nosing round the ruins this morning soon after breakfast (he hides things to eat there) and turned on all the Northern Lights for two years in one go. You have never heard or seen anything like it. I have tried to draw a picture of it; but I am too shaky to do it properly and you can't paint fizzing light can you?

I think the Polar Bear has spoilt the picture rather – of course he can't draw with those great fat paws –

Rude! I can – and write without shaking.

by going and putting a bit of his own about me chasing the reindeer and him laughing. He did laugh too. So did I when I saw him trying to draw reindeer, and inking his nice white paws.

Father Christmas had to hurry away and leave me to finish. He is old and gets worried when funny things happen. You would have laughed too! I think it is good of me laughing. It was a lovely firework. The reindeer will run quick to England this year. They are still frightened!…

Christmas
1926

Cliff House
Top of the World
Near the NORTH POLE
Monday Dec. 1926 20th

My dear boys,

I am more shaky than usual this year. The North Polar Bear's fault! It was the biggest bang in the world, & the most monstrous firework there ever has been. It turned the North Pole BLACK & shook all the stars out of place, broke the moon into four — and the Man in it fell into my back garden. He ate quite a lot of my Xmas chocolates before he said he felt better & climbed back to mend it and get the stars tidy. Then I found out that the reindeer had broken loose. They were running all over the country, breaking reins and ropes & tossing presents up in the air. They were all packed up to start, you see, — yes it only happened this morning: it was a sleigh load of chocolate things — which I always send to England early. Those yours are not badly damaged. But isn't the N.P.B. silly? And he isn't a bit sorry! Of course he did it — you remember I had to move last year because of him? The tap for turning on the Rory Bory Aylis fireworks is still in the cellar of my old house. The N.P.B. knew he must never never touch it. I only let it off on special days like Christmas. He says he thought it was cut off since we moved — anyway he was nosing round the ruins this morning soon after breakfast (he hides things to eat there) and turned on all the Northern Lights for two years in one go. You have never heard or seen anything like it. I have tried to draw a picture of it; but I am too shaky to do it properly and you can't paint fizzing light can you?

I think the P.B. has spoilt the picture rather — of course he can't draw with those great fat paws — by going and putting a bit of his own about me chasing the reindeer and him laughing. He did laugh too. So did I when I saw him.

rude. NPB
I can — and write
without shaking

PTO

27

trying to draw reindeer, and inking his nice white paws

FATHER X. had to hurry away and leave me to finish. He is old and gets worried when funny things happen. You would have laughed too! I think it is good of me laughing. It was a lovely firework.

The reindeer will run quick to England this year. They are still frightened!

I must go and help pack. I don't know what F.C would do without me. He always forgets what a lot of packing I do for him.

The Snow Man is addressing our envelopes this year. He is F.C's gardener – but we don't get much but snowdrops and frost-ferns to grow here. He always writes in white, just with his finger.

A merry Christmas to you from. NPB.

And love from Father Christmas to you all.

I must go and help pack. I don't know what Father Christmas would do without me. He always forgets what a lot of packing I do for him...

The Snow Man is addressing our envelopes this year. He is Father Christmas's gardener – but we don't get much but snowdrops and frost-ferns to grow here. He always writes in white, just with his finger...

A merry Christmas to you from North Polar Bear

And love from Father Christmas to you all.

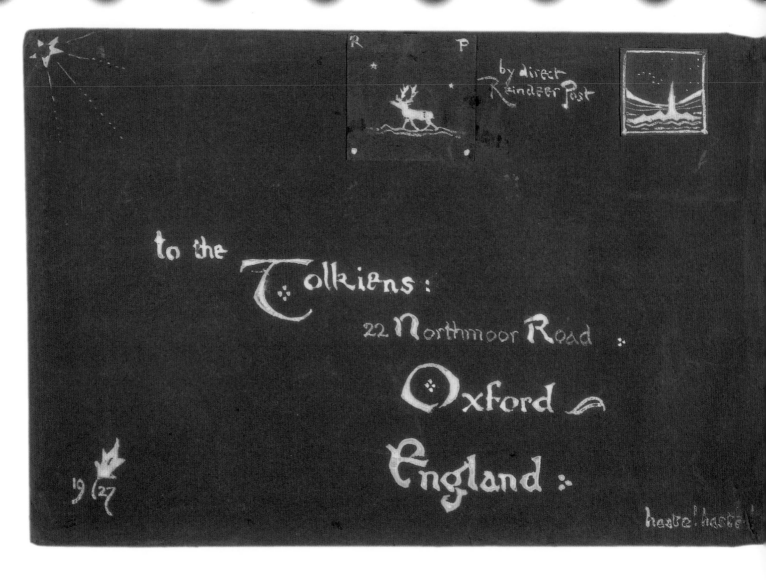

to the

Tolkiens:

22 Northmoor Road :.

Oxford

England :.

by direct
Reindeer Post

R   P

19/27

haste! haste!

Very Sorry — am sending this off to night
(Friday): Polar B forgot to post it.
It must go by special Reindeer
which needs

Special Stamp
F.C.
Should get to you on Xmas
morning .....

My dear people—:

Cliff House, Top o'the World, near the North Pole
Wednesday December 21st 1927

My dear people: there seem to get more and more of you every year.

I get poorer and poorer: still I hope that I have managed to bring you all something you wanted, though not everything you asked for (Michael and Christopher! I haven't heard from John this year. I suppose he is growing too big and won't even hang up his stocking soon).

It has been so bitter at the North Pole lately that the North Polar Bear has spent most of the time asleep and has been less use than usual this Christmas.

Everybody does sleep most of the time here in winter – especially Father Christmas.

The North Pole became colder than any cold thing ever has been, and when the North Polar Bear put his nose against it – took the skin off: now it is bandaged with red flannel. Why did he? I don't know, but he is always putting his nose where it oughtn't to be – into my cupboards for instance.

That's because I am hungry

Also it has been very dark here since winter began. We haven't seen the Sun, of course, for three months, but there are no Northern Lights this year – you remember the awful accident last year? There will be none again until the end of 1928. The North Polar Bear has got his cousin (and distant friend) the Great Bear to shine extra bright for us, and this week I have hired a comet to do my packing by, but it doesn't work as well.

The North Polar Bear has not really been any more sensible this year:

I have been perfectly sensible, and have learnt to write with a pen in my mouth instead of a paintbrush.

Yesterday he was snowballing the Snow Man in the garden and pushed him over the edge of the cliff so that he fell into my sleigh at the bottom and broke lots of things – one of them was himself. I used some of what was left of him to paint my white picture. We shall have to make ourselves a new gardener when we are less busy.

The Man in the Moon paid me a visit the other day – a fortnight ago exactly – he often does about this time, as he gets lonely in the Moon, and we make him a nice little Plum Pudding (he is so fond of things with plums in!)

His fingers were cold as usual, and the North Polar Bear made him play 'snapdragons' to warm them. Of course he burnt them, and then he licked them, and then he liked the brandy, and then the Bear gave him lots more, and he went fast asleep on the sofa. Then I went down into the cellars to make crackers, and he rolled off the sofa, and the wicked bear pushed him underneath and forgot all about him! He can never be away a whole night from the moon; but he was this time.

I have never been expected to look after the Man in the Moon before. I was very nice to him, and he was very comfy under the sofa.

Suddenly the Snow Man (he wasn't broken then) rushed in out of the garden, next day just after teatime, and said the moon was going out! The dragons had come out and were making an awful smoke and smother. We rolled him out and shook him and he simply whizzed back, but it was ages before he got things quite cleared up.

I believe he had to let loose one of his simply terrificalest freezing magics before he could drive the dragons back into their holes, and that is why it has got so cold down here.

The Polar Bear only laughs when I tell him it's his fault, and he curls up on my hearthrug and won't do anything but snore.

My messengers told me that you have somebody from Iceland staying with you. That is not so far from where I live, and nearly as cold. People don't hang up stockings there, and I usually pass by in a hurry, though I sometimes pop down and leave a thing or two for their very jolly Christmas Trees.

My usual way is down through Norway, Denmark, Germany, Switzerland, and then back through Germany, Northern France, Belgium, and so into England: and on the way home I pass over the sea, and sometimes Iceland and I can see the twinkling lights faint in the valleys under their mountains. But I go by quick, as my reindeer gallop as hard as they can there – they always say they are frightened a volcano or a geyser will go off underneath them.

This must be all: I have written you a very long letter this year as there was nothing to draw, but dark and snow and stars.

Love to you all, and happiness next year.

Your loving Father Christmas

These are blots which Fr Ch. could not help not !!

I believe he had to let loose one of his simplest terrificalest freezing magics before he could drive the dragons back into their holes, and that is why it has got so cold down here. The Polar Bear only laughs when I tell him it is his fault, & he curls up on my hearthrug & wont do anything but snore.

My messengers told me that you have somebody from Iceland staying with you. That is not so far from where I live & nearly as cold. People dont hang up stockings there, & usually pass by in a hurry, though I sometimes pop down and leave a thing or two for their very jolly Christmas Trees. My usual way is down through Norway, Denmark, Germany, Switzerland, and then back through Germany, Northern France, Belgium, Holland & into England, & on the way home I pass over the sea, and sometimes Iceland, & I can see the twinkling lights faint in the valleys under their mountains. But I go by quick as my reindeer gallop as hard as they can there — they always say they are frightened a volcano or a geysir will go off underneath them.

This must be all: I have written you a very long letter this year to make up for the "dark" card — I there was nothing to draw, but dark & snow and stars. Love to you all, and happiness NEXT Year

Your loving

Father Christmas

* 5. This is Fr Christ-
mas's hearthrug and I
am not on it. NPB

like that

My notes. NPB.

* 1 of course you know! and everybody does sleep most of the time here in winter — especially Fr Ch.

* 2. That's because I am hungry

* 3 I have been perfectly sensible, and have learnt to write with a pen in my mouth instead of a paintbrush.

* 4 I have never been expected to look after the man in the Moone before. I was very nice to him, & he was very comfy under the sofa.

"Top o' the World" North Pole

Top o' the World, North Pole
Thursday December 20th 1928

My dear boys,

Another Christmas and I am another year older – and so are you. I feel quite well all the same – very nice of Michael to ask – and not quite so shaky. But that is because we have got all the lighting and heating right again after the cold dark year we had in 1927 – you remember about it?

And I expect you remember whose fault it was? What do you think the poor dear old bear has been and done this time? Nothing as bad as letting off all the lights. Only fell from top to bottom of the main stairs on Thursday!

Who'd left the soap on the stairs? Not me!

We were beginning to get the first lot of parcels down out of the storerooms into the hall. Polar Bear would insist on taking an enormous pile on his head as well as lots in his arms. Bang Rumble Clatter Crash! Awful moanings and growlings.

I ran out on to the landing and saw he had fallen from top to bottom on to his nose leaving a trail of balls, bundles, parcels and things all the way down – and he had fallen on top of some and smashed them. I hope you got none of these by accident? I have drawn you a picture of it all. Polar Bear was rather grumpy at my drawing it:

1928
~
~

Your loving ☆ ✦ ✦ ✦

Father Christmas

Of course, naturally.

He says my Christmas pictures always make fun of him and that one year he will send one drawn by himself of me being idiotic (but of course I never am, and he can't draw well enough).

Yes I can. I drew the flag at the end.

He joggled my arm and spoilt the little picture at the bottom of the moon laughing and Polar Bear shaking his fist at it.

When he had picked himself up he ran out of doors and wouldn't help clear up because I sat on the stairs and laughed as soon as I found there was not much damage done – that is why the moon smiled: but the part showing Polar Bear angry was cut off because he smudged it.

But anyway I thought you would like a picture of the inside of my new big house for a change. The chief hall is under the largest dome, where we pile the presents usually ready to load on the sleighs at the doors. Polar Bear and I built it nearly all ourselves, and laid all the blue and mauve tiles. The banisters and roof are not quite straight…

Not my fault. Father Christmas did the banisters.

…but it doesn't really matter. I painted pictures on the walls of the trees and stars and suns and moons. Then I said to Polar Bear, "I shall leave the frieze (F. R. I. E. Z. E) to you."

He said, "I should have thought there was enough freeze outside – and your colours inside, all purply-grey-y-bluey-pale greeny are cold enough too."

I said, "Don't be a silly bear: do your best, there's a good old polar" – and what

8

"Top o' the World"
NORTH POLE
Thursday December 20th
1928

My Dear Boys

ANOTHER CHRISTMAS and I am another year older—and so are you. I feel quite well all the same—very nice of MICHAEL to ask—and not quite so shaky. But that is because we have got all the lighting and heating right again after the cold dark year we had in 1927—you remember about it? And I expect you remember whose fault it was? What do you think the poor dear old bear has been and done this time? Nothing as bad as letting off all the lights. Only fell from top to bottom of the main stairs on Thursday! We were beginning to get the first lot of parcels down out of the storerooms into the hall. PB would insist on taking an enormous pile on his head as well as lots in his arms. Bang Rumble Clatter Crash! awful moanings and growlings: I ran out on to the landing and saw he had fallen from top to bottom onto his nose—leaving a trail of balls bundles parcels & things all the way down—and he had fallen on top of some and smashed them. I hope you got none of these by accident? I have drawn you a picture of it all. PB was rather grumpy at my drawing it: he says my Christmas pictures always make fun of him & that one year he will send one drawn by himself of me being idiotic (but of course I never am, and he can't draw well enough). He joggled my arm and spoilt the little picture at the bottom, of the moon

WHO LEFT THE SOAP ON THE STARES? NOT ME!

OF COURSE NATURALY

YES I CAN
I DREW FLAG AT END.

a result!! Icicles all round the hall to make a freeze (F. R. E. E. Z.E.) (he can't spell very well), and fearful bright colour to make a warm freeze!!!

Well, my dears, I hope you will like the things I am bringing: nearly all you asked for and lots of other little things you didn't, and which I thought of at the last minute. I hope you will share the railway things and farm and animals often, and not think they are absolutely only for the one whose stocking they were in. Take care of them, for they are some of my very best things.

Love to Chris: love to Michael: love to John who must be getting very big as he doesn't write to me any more (so I simply had to guess paints – I hope they were all right: Polar Bear chose them; he says he knows what John likes because John likes bears).

Your loving Father Christmas

And my love, Polar Bear

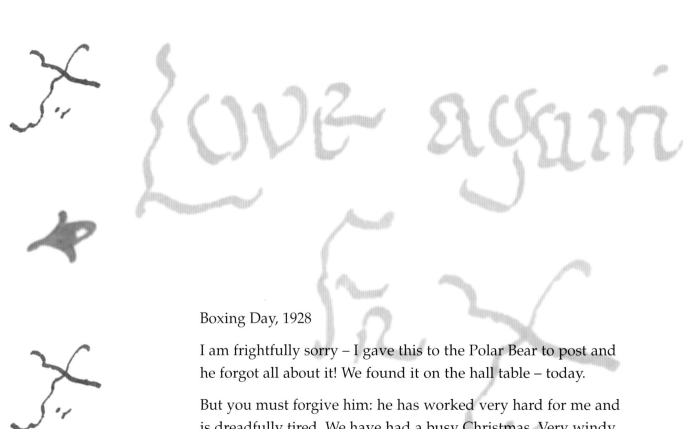

Boxing Day, 1928

I am frightfully sorry – I gave this to the Polar Bear to post and he forgot all about it! We found it on the hall table – today.

But you must forgive him: he has worked very hard for me and is dreadfully tired. We have had a busy Christmas. Very windy here. It blew several sleighs over before they could start.

Love again, Father Christmas

9

BOXING DAY
1928

I am frightfully
sorry —— I gave
this to the P B to
post and he forgot
all about it! We
found it on the hall
table to day.

But you must forgive
him: he has worked
very hard for me & is
dreadfully tired. We
have had a busy Christ-
mas. Very windy here:
It blew several sleighs
over before they could
start——

Love again

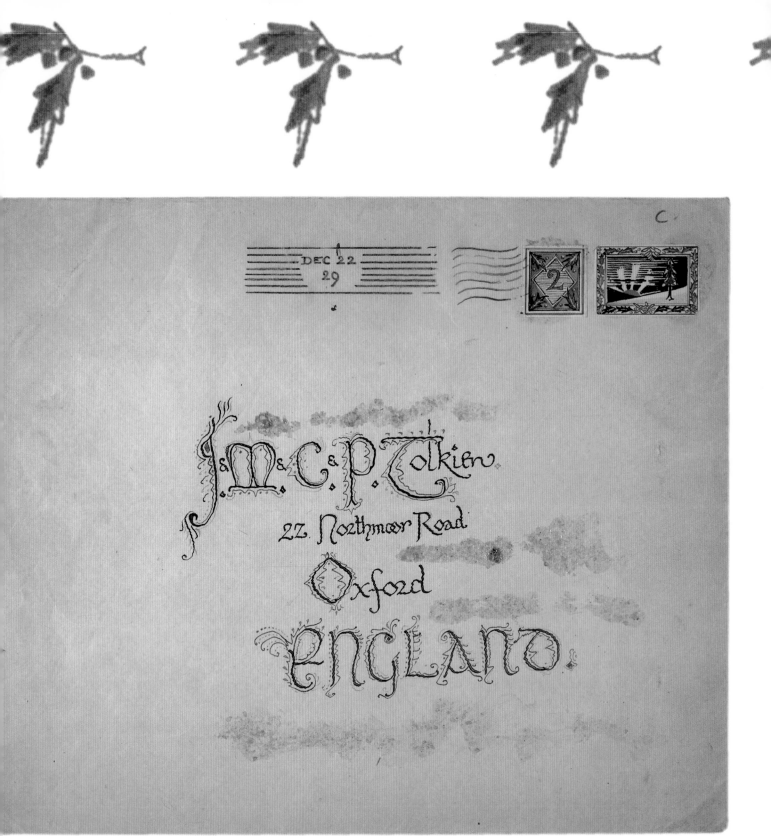

J. & M. & C. & P. Tolkien

22. Northmoor Road

Oxford

ENGLAND.

England, Norway Denmark

1929

Sweden & Germany.

November 1929

Dear boys,

My paw is better. I was cutting Christmas trees when I hurt it. Don't you think my writing is much better too? Father Christmas is very bisy already. So am I. We have had hevy snow and sum of our messengers got buerried and sum lost: that is whi you have not herd lately.

Love to John for his birthday. Father Christmas says my English spelling is not good. I kant help it. We don't speak English here, only Arktik (which you dont know. We also make our letters different – I have made mine like Arktik letters for you to see. We always rite ↑ for T and V for U. This is sum Arktik langwidge wich means "Goodby till I see you next and I hope it will bee soon." – Mára mesta an ni véla tye ento, ya rato nea.

P. B.

My real name is Karhu but I dont tell most peeple.

P.S. I like letters and think Cristofers are nice

P.S. I LIKE LETTERS AND THINK
CRISTOFERS AR NICE.

15

DEAR BOYS

NOV 1929

MY PAW IS BETTER   I WAS CUTTING CHRISTMAS
TREES WEN I HURT IT. DON'T YOU THINK MY WRITING
IS MUCH BETTER TOO?   FATHER X IS VERY BISY
ALREADY. SO AM I WE HAVE HAD HEVY SNOW AND
SUM OF OUR MESSENGERS GOT BUERRIED AND SUM
LOST: THAT IS WHI YOU HAVE NOT HERD LATELY.
LOVE TO JOHN FOR HIS BIRTHDAY   FATHER X SAYS
MI ENGLISH SPELLING IS NOT GOOD. I KANT HELP IT. WE
DON'T SPEAK ENGLISH HERE, ONLY ARKTIK (WHICH YOU

DON'T KNOW. WE ALSO MAKE OUR LETTERS DIFFERENT
∾ I HAVE MADE MINE LIKE ARKTIK LETTERS FOR YOU TO
SEE. WE ALWAYS RITE ↑ FOR T AND V FOR U.
THIS IS SUM ARKTIK LANGWIDGE WICH MEANS
"GOOD BY TILL I SEE YOU NEXT AND I HOPE IT
WILL BEE SOON." ∾∾ MARA MESTA AN NI VELA TYE
ENTO, YA RANO NEA

P.B.

MY REAL NAME IS KARHU BUT I DON'T TELL
MOST PEEPLE.

MI PAW

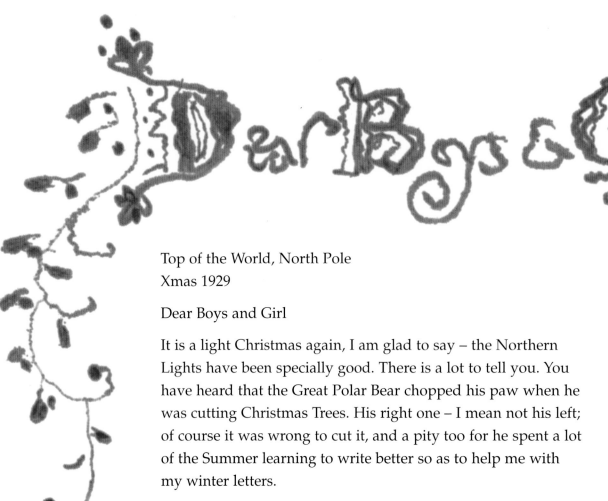

Top of the World, North Pole
Xmas 1929

Dear Boys and Girl

It is a light Christmas again, I am glad to say – the Northern Lights have been specially good. There is a lot to tell you. You have heard that the Great Polar Bear chopped his paw when he was cutting Christmas Trees. His right one – I mean not his left; of course it was wrong to cut it, and a pity too for he spent a lot of the Summer learning to write better so as to help me with my winter letters.

We had a Bonfire this year (to please the Polar Bear) to celebrate the coming in of winter. The Snow-elves let off all the rockets together, which surprised us both. I have tried to draw you a picture of it, but really there were hundreds of rockets. You can't see the elves at all against the snow background.

The Bonfire made a hole in the ice and woke up the Great Seal, who happened to be underneath. The Polar Bear let off 20,000 silver sparklers afterwards – used up all my stock, so that is why I had none to send you. Then he went for a holiday!!! – to north Norway, and stayed with a wood-cutter called Olaf, and came back with paw all bandaged just at the beginning of our busy times.

There seem more children than ever in England, Norway, Denmark, Sweden, and Germany, which are the countries I specially look after (and of course North America and Canada) – not to speak of getting stuff down to the South Pole for children who expect to be looked after though they have gone to live in New Zealand or Australia or South Africa or China. It

Great Polar Bear

is a good thing clocks don't tell the same time all over the world or I should never get round, although when my magic is strongest – at Christmas – I can do about a thousand stockings a minute, if I have it all planned out beforehand. You could hardly guess the enormous piles of lists I make out. I seldom get them mixed.

But I am rather worried this year. In my office and packing-room, the Polar Bear reads out names while I copy them down. We had awful gales here, worse than you did, tearing clouds of snow to a million tatters, screaming like demons, burying my house almost up to the roofs. Just at the worst, the Polar Bear said it was stuffy! and opened a north window before I could stop him. You can guess the result – the North Polar Bear was buried in papers and lists; but that did not stop him laughing.

Also all my red and green ink was upset, as well as black, – so I am writing in chalk and pencil. I have some black ink left, and the Polar Bear is using it to address parcels.

I liked all your letters – very much indeed my dears. Nobody, or very few, write so much or so nicely to me. I'm specially pleased with Christopher's card, and his letters, and with his

Christmas Trees.

learning to write, so I am sending him a fountain pen and also a special picture for himself. It shows me crossing the sea on the upper North wind, while a South West gale – reindeer hate it – is raising big waves below.

This must be all now. I send you all my love. One more stocking to fill this year! I hope you will like your new house and the things I bring you.

Your Old Father Christmas

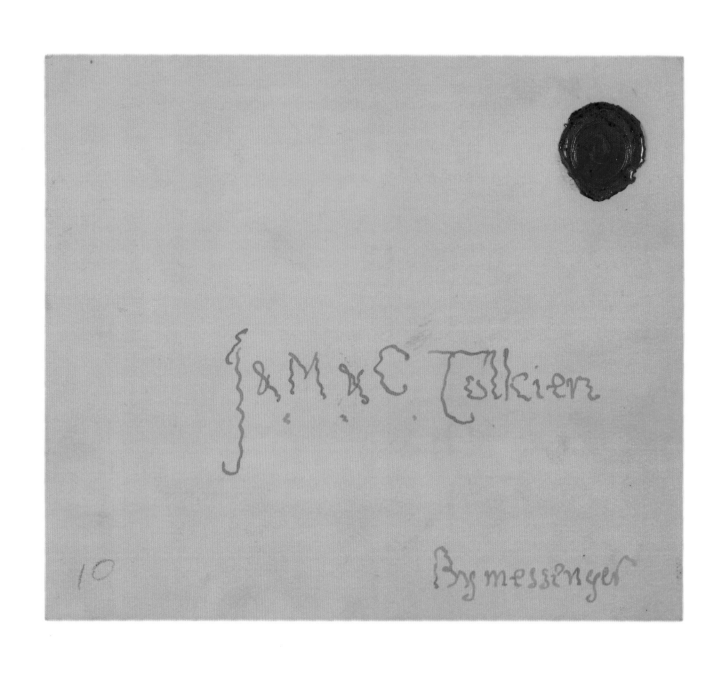

J & M & C Tolkien

10

By messenger

1930

Fr Christmas

> *Nov 28th 1930.*
>
> *Fr Christmas has got all your letters! What a lot, especially from C & M! Thank you, and also Reddy and your bears, & other animals.*
>
> *I am just beginning to get awfully busy. Let me know more about what you specially want. Also (if you can find out) what anyone else like P or Mummy or Auntie (I mean C Miss) Grove wants. P.B sends love. He is just getting better. He has had whooping Cough!! F.N.C.*

November 28th 1930

Father Christmas has got all your letters! What a lot, especially from Christopher and Michael! Thank you, and also Reddy and your bears, and other animals.

I am just beginning to get awfully busy. Let me know more about what you specially want.

Polar Bear sends love. He is just getting better. He has had Whooping Cough!!

Father Nicholas Christmas

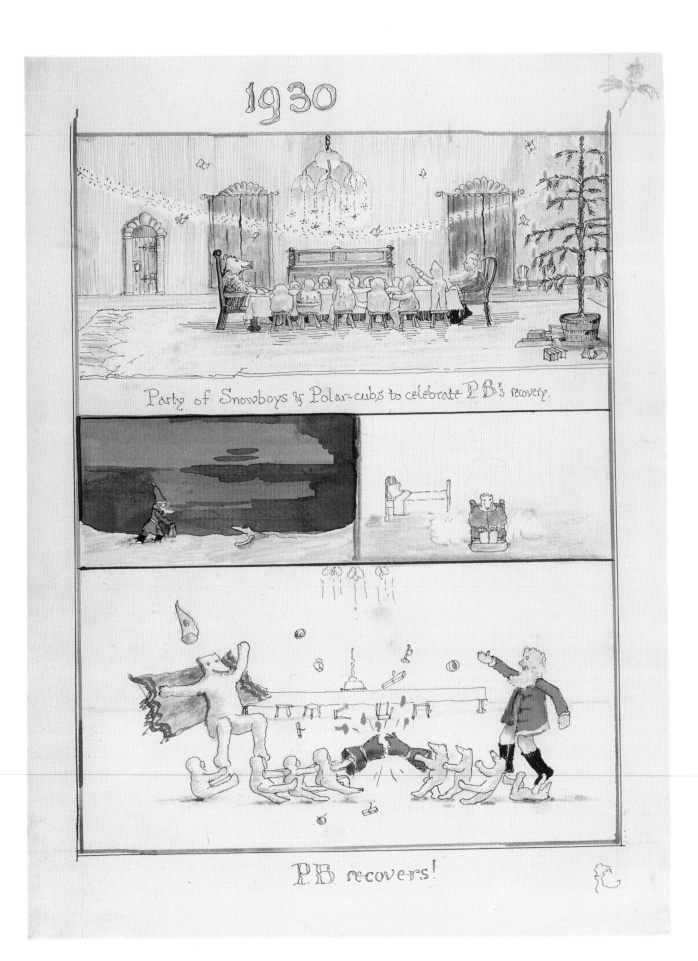

1930

Party of Snowboys & Polar-cubs to celebrate P.B's recovery.

P.B recovers!

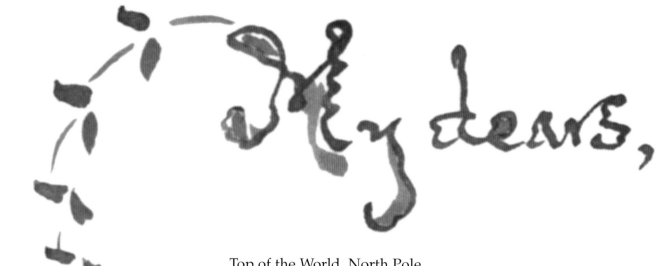

Top of the World, North Pole
Christmas 1930
Not finished until Christmas Eve, 24th December

My dears,

I have enjoyed all your letters. I am dreadfully sorry there has been no time to answer them, and even now I have not time to finish my picture for you properly or to send you a full long letter like I mean to.

I hope you will like your stockings this year: I tried to find what you asked for, but the stores have been in rather a muddle – you see the Polar Bear has been ill. He had whooping cough first of all. I could not let him help with the packing and sorting which begins in November – because it would be simply awful if any of my children caught Polar whooping cough and barked like bears on Boxing Day. So I had to do everything myself in the preparations.

Of course, Polar Bear has done his best – he cleaned up and mended my sleigh, and looked after the reindeer while I was busy. That is how the really bad accident happened. Early this month we had a most awful snowstorm (nearly six feet of snow) followed by an awful fog. The poor Polar Bear went out to the reindeer-stables, and got lost and nearly buried: I did not miss him or go to look for him for a long while. His chest had not got well from whooping cough so this made him frightfully ill, and he was in bed until three days ago. Everything has gone wrong, and there has been no one to look after my messengers properly.

Aren't you glad the Polar Bear is better? We had a party of Snowboys (sons of the Snowmen, which are the only sort of people that live near – not of course men made of snow, though my gardener who is the oldest of all the snowmen sometimes draws a picture of a made Snowman instead of writing his name) and Polar Cubs (the Polar Bear's nephews) on Saturday as soon as he felt well enough.

He didn't eat much tea, but when the big cracker went off after, he threw away his rug, and leaped in the air and has been well ever since.

I've drawn you pictures of everything that happened – Polar Bear telling a story after all the tea things had been cleared away; me finding Polar Bear in the snow, and Polar Bear sitting with his feet in hot mustard and water to stop him shivering. It didn't – and he sneezed so terribly he blew five candles out.

Still he is all right now – I know because he has been at his tricks again: quarrelling with the Snowman (my gardener) and pushing him through the roof of his snow house; and packing lumps of ice instead of presents in naughty children's parcels. That might be a good idea, only he never told me and some of them (with ice) were put in warm storerooms and melted all over good children's presents!

Well my dears there is lots more I should like to say – about my green brother and my father, old Grandfather Yule, and why we were both called Nicholas after the Saint (whose day is December sixth) who used to give secret presents, sometimes throwing purses of money through the window. But I must hurry away – I am late already and I am afraid you may not get this in time.

Kisses to you all,

Father Nicholas Christmas

P.S. (Chris has no need to be frightened of me).

Your Loving Father Christmas

I AM SO
SORRY I FOR
GOT TO POST
THIS. LOVE
KARHU

1931

J.F.R & M.H.R & C.R & P.M.R
TOLKIEN.
20 Northmoor Road: Oxford. England.

URGENT.

By flying messenger please N.C.

My dear Children.

59

My latest portrait. — Father Christmas packing 1931. Love to you all. Your loving F.C. N.C.

Cliff House
October 31st 1931

Dear Children,

Already I have got some letters from you! You are getting busy early. I have not begun to think about Christmas yet. It has been very warm in the North this year, and there has been very little snow so far. We are just getting in our Christmas firewood.

This is just to say my messengers will be coming round regularly now Winter has begun – we shall be having a bonfire

Cliff House
Oct. 31
1931

Dear Children,

Already I have got
some letters from you!
You are getting busy early. I
have not begun to think about
Christmas yet. It has been very
warm in the North this year, &
there has been very little snow so
far. We are just getting in
our Xmas fire wood.

This is just to say my messengers
will be coming round regularly now.

tomorrow – and I shall like to hear from you: Sunday and Wednesday evenings are the best times to post to me.

The Polar Bear is quite well and fairly good – (though you never know what he will do when the Christmas rush begins.) Send my love to John.

Your loving
Father Nicholas Christmas

Glad Father Christmas has wakt up. He slept nearly all this hot summer. I wish we kood have snow. My coat is quite yellow.

Love Polar Bear

Winter has begun — We shall be having a bonfire tomorrow — & I shall like to hear from you: Sunday & Wednesday evenings are the best times to post to me.

The P.B. is quite well & fairly good — though you never know what he will do when the Xmas rush begins. Send my love to John.

Yr loving

Frs Xmas

GLAD FR X HAS WAKT VP. HE SLEPT NEARLY ALL THIS HOT SVMMER. I WISH WE KOOD HAVE SNOW. MY COAT IS QVITE YELLOW. LOVE. P.B.

Cliff House, North Pole
December 23rd 1931

My dear Children

I hope you will like the little things I have sent you. You seem to be most interested in Railways just now, so I am sending you mostly things of that sort. I send as much love as ever, in fact more. We have both, the old Polar Bear and I, enjoyed having so many nice letters from you and your pets. If you think we have not read them you are wrong; but if you find that not many of the things you asked for have come, and not perhaps quite as many as sometimes, remember that this Christmas all over the world there are a terrible number of poor and starving people.

I (and also my Green Brother) have had to do some collecting of food and clothes, and toys too, for the children whose fathers and mothers and friends cannot give them anything, sometimes not even dinner. I know yours won't forget you.

So, my dears, I hope you will be happy this Christmas and not quarrel, and will have some good games with your Railway all together. Don't forget old Father Christmas, when you light your tree.

Nor me!

It has gone on being warm up here as I told you – not what you would call warm, but warm for the North Pole, with very little snow. The North Polar Bear, if you know who I mean, has been lazy and sleepy as a result, and very slow over packing, or any job except eating. He has enjoyed sampling and tasting the food parcels this year (to see if they were fresh and good, he said).

Somebody haz to – and I found stones in some of the kurrants.

But that is not the worst – I should hardly feel it was Christmas if he didn't do something ridiculous. You will never guess what he did this time! I sent him down into one of my cellars – the Cracker-hole we call it – where I keep thousands of boxes of crackers (you would like to see them, rows upon rows, all with their lids off to show the kinds of colours).

Well, I wanted 20 boxes, and was busy sorting soldiers and farm things, so I sent him; and he was so lazy he took two Snowboys (who aren't allowed down there) to help him. They started pulling crackers out of boxes, and he tried to box them (the boys' ears I mean), and they dodged and he fell over, and let his candle fall right POOF! into my firework crackers and boxes of sparklers.

I could hear the noise, and smell the smell in the hall; and when I rushed down I saw nothing but smoke and fizzing stars, and old Polar Bear was rolling over on the

64

Cliff House.
North Pole.
December 23rd 1931.

My dear Children.

I hope you will like the little things I have sent you.
You seem to be most interested in Railways just now, so I
am sending you mostly things of that sort. I send as much love as
ever, in fact more. We have both, the old P.B. and I, enjoyed
having so many nice letters from you and your pets. If you think we
have not read them you are wrong; but if you find that not many of
the things you asked for have come, & not perhaps quite as
many as sometimes, remember that this Christmas all over the
world there are a terrible number of poor & starving people.
Also my Green Brothers have had to do some collecting of food &
clothes, and toys too, for the children whose fathers & mothers and friends
cannot give them anything, sometimes not even dinner. I know yours
wont forget you. So, my dears, I hope you will be happy this Xmas
& not quarrel, & will have some good games with your Railway all
together. Don't forget old Father Christmas, when you light your tree *

It has gone on being warm up here as I told you — not what
you would very call warm, but warm for the N. Pole, with
very little snow. The N.P.B., if you know who I mean ** has SILLY
been lazy & sleepy as a result, & very slow over packing, or any job except eating — he has enjoyed sampling and tasting the food parcels, this
† year (to see if they were fresh & good, he said). But that is
not the worst — I should hardly feel it was Christmas, if he didn't
do something ridiculous. You will never guess what he did this time! I
sent him down into one of my cellars — the Cracker-hole we call it
where I keep thousands of boxes of crackers (you would like to see them,
rows upon rows, all with their lids off to show the kinds & colours) —
well, I wanted 20 boxes, & was busy sorting soldiers & farm things,

NOR
ME.N.
P.B!

† SOMEBODY HAZ TO — AND I FOUND STONES IN SOME OF THE KURRANTS

floor with sparks sizzling in his coat: he has quite a bare patch burnt on his back.

It looked fine!
That's where Father Christmas spilled the gravy on my back at dinner!

The Snowboys roared with laughter and then ran away. They said it was a splendid sight – but they won't come to my party on St Stephen's Day; they have had more than their share already.

Two of the Polar Bear's nephews have been staying here for some time – Paksu and Valkotukka ('fat' and 'white-hair' they say it means). They are fat-tummied polar-cubs, and are very funny boxing one another and rolling about. But another time, I shall have them on Boxing Day, and not just at packing-time. I fell over them fourteen times a day last week.

And Valkotukka swallowed a ball of red string, thinking it was cake, and he got it all wound up inside and had a tangled cough – he couldn't sleep at night, but I thought it rather served him right for putting holly in my bed.

It was the same cub that poured all the black ink yesterday into the fire – to make night: it did and a very smelly smoky one. We lost Paksu all last Wednesday and found him on Thursday morning asleep in a cupboard in the kitchen; he had eaten two whole puddings raw. They seem to be growing up just like their uncle.

Not fair!

Goodbye now. I shall soon be off on my travels once more. You need not believe any pictures you see of me in aeroplanes or motors. I cannot drive one, and don't want to; and they are too slow anyway (not to mention smell). They cannot compare with my own reindeer, which I train myself. They are all very well this year, and I expect my posts will be in very good time. I have got some new young ones this Christmas from Lapland (a great place for wizards; but these are WHIZZERS).

Bad!

One day I will send you a picture of my deer-stables and harness-houses. I am expecting that John, although he is now over 14, will hang up his stocking this last time; but I don't forget people even when they are past stocking-age, not until they forget me. So I send LOVE to you ALL, and especially little PM, who is beginning her stocking-days and I hope they will be happy.

Your loving Father Christmas

P.S. This is all drawn by North Polar Bear. Don't you think he is getting better? But the green ink is mine – and he didn't ask for it.

So I sent him; and he was so lazy he took two Snow-boys (who aren't allowed down there) to help him. They started pulling crackers out of boxes, and he tried to box them (the boys' ears I mean), and they dodged and he fell over, & let his candle fall right poof! into my fire-work crackers, & boxes of sparklers. I could hear the noise, & smell the smell, in the hall; & when I rushed down I saw nothing but smoke and fizzing stars, & old P.B. was rolling over on the floor with sparks sizzling in his coat: he has quite a bare patch burnt on his back ✱. The Snow-boys roared with laughter & then ran away. They said it was a splendid sight, but they won't come to my party on St Stephen's Day; they have had more than their share already.

THAT'S WHERE F.C. SPILLED THE GRAVY ON MY BACK AT DINNER!

IT LOOKED FINE

Two of the P.B.'s nephews have been staying there for some time — Paksu and Valkotukka ("fat" and "white-hair" they say it means). They are fat-tummied polar-cubs, & are very funny boxing one another, & rolling about. But another time, I shall have them on Boxing-day & not just at packing-time. I fell over them fourteen times a day last week. And Valkotukka swallowed a ball of red string, thinking it was cake, and he got it all wound up inside and had a tangled cough — he couldn't sleep at night, but I thought it rather served him right for putting holly in my bed. It was the same cub that poured all the black ink yesterday into the fire — to make night': it did & a very smelly smoky one. We lost Paksu all last Wednesday & found him on Thursday morning asleep in a cupboard in the kitchen; he had eaten two whole pudd-ings raw. They seem to be growing up just like their uncle.

NOT FAIR!

Good-bye now. I shall soon be off on my travels once more. You need not believe any pictures you see of me in aeroplanes or motors. I cannot drive one, & I don't want to; and they are too slow anyway (not to mention smell), they cannot compare with my own reindeer, which I train myself. They are all very well this year, & I expect my posts will be in very good time. I have got some new young ones this Christ-mas from Lapland (a great place for wizards; but these are WHIZZERS) One day I will send you a picture of my deer-stables and harness-houses.

BAD!

I am expecting that John, although he is now over 14, will hang up his stock-ing this last time; but I don't forget people even when they are past stocking-age, not until they forget me. So I send LOVE to you ALL, & espec-ially little P.M., who is beginning her stocking-days, & I hope they will be happy.

Your loving Father Christmas

1931 −32

N.P.B.   KARHU

LOVE FROM KARHU, PAKSU, AND VALKOTUKKA.   V

This is all drawn by N.P.B. Don't you think he's getting better. But the green ink is mine — if he didn't ask for it.

Ma making
pastry

?B very
busy helping.

Rough sketch of cracker accident. I had no
time to do proper picture.

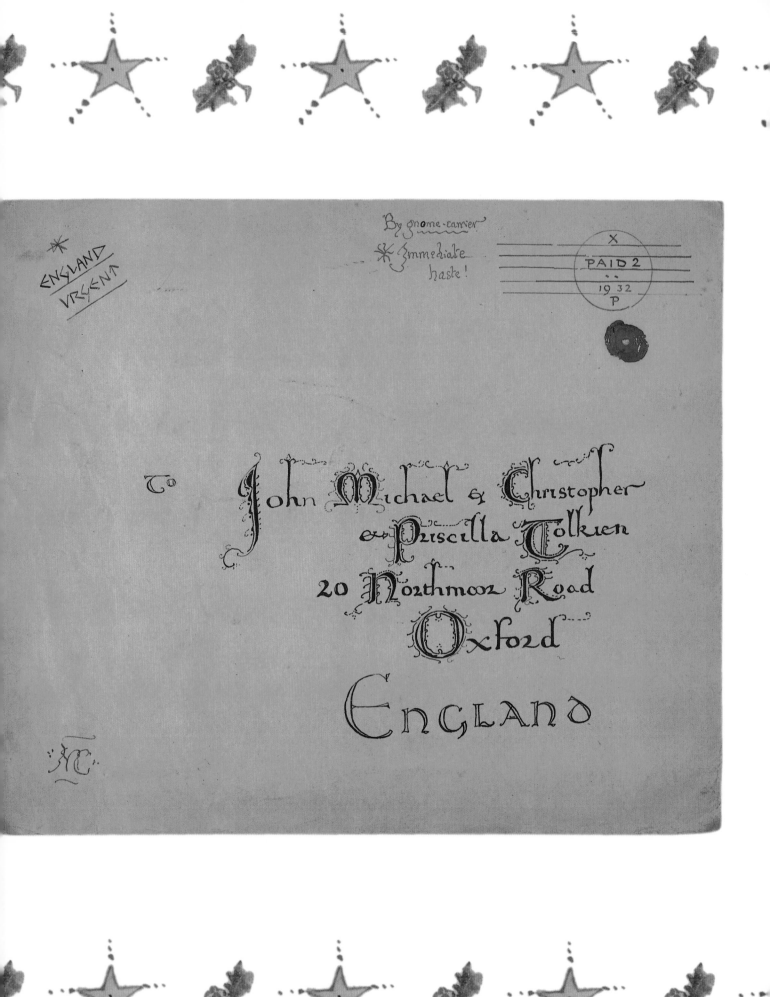

By gnome-carrier
✳ Immediate
haste!

X
PAID 2
··
19 32
P

ENGLAND
VRGENT

To John Michael & Christopher
& Priscilla Tolkien
20 Northmoor Road
Oxford

ENGLAND

1932

NC

Cliff House, North Pole.
November 30th 1932

My dear children

Thank you for your nice letters. I have not forgotten you. I am very late this year and very worried – a very funny thing has happened. The Polar Bear has disappeared, and I don't know where he is. I have not seen him since the beginning of this month, and I am getting anxious. Tomorrow December, the Christmas month, begins, and I don't know what I shall do without him.

I am glad you are all well and your many pets. The Snowbabies holidays begin tomorrow. I wish Polar Bear was here to look after them. Love to Michael, Christopher and Priscilla. Please send John my love when you write to him.

Father Christmas.

Cliff House
North Pole.

November 30th
.1932.

 My dear Children

Thank you for your nice letters. I have
not forgotten you. I am very late this year, & very
worried—a very funny thing has happened. The
P.B. has disappeared, & I don't know where he
is. I have not seen him since the beginning of this
month, & I am getting anxious. Tomorrow December, the Christmas month, begins, & I don't
know what I shall do without him.

I am glad you are all well, & your many
pets.   The snow babies holidays begin tomorrow.
I wish P.B was here to look after them. Love
to M. C. & P.   Please send J. my love when you
write to him.
                    Father N. Christmas.

73

Cliff House, near the North Pole
December 23rd 1932

My dear children,

There is a lot to tell you. First of all a Merry Christmas! But there have been lots of adventures you will want to hear about. It all began with the funny noises underground which started in the summer and got worse and worse. I was afraid an earthquake might happen. The North Polar Bear says he suspected what was wrong from the beginning. I only wish he had said something to me; and anyway it can't be quite true, as he was fast asleep when it began, and did not wake up till about Michael's birthday.

However, he went off for a walk one day, at the end of November I think, and never came back! About a fortnight ago I began to be really worried, for after all the dear old thing is really a lot of help, in spite of accidents, and very amusing.

One Friday evening (December 9th) there was a bumping at the front door, and a snuffling. I thought he had come back, and lost his key (as often before); but when I opened the door there was another very old bear there, a very fat and funny-shaped one. Actually it was the eldest of the few remaining cave-bears, old Mr Cave Bear himself (I had not seen him for centuries).

"Do you want your North Polar Bear?" he said. "If you do you had better come and get him!" It turned out he was lost in the caves (belonging to Mr Cave Bear, or so he says) not far from the ruins of my old house. He says he found a hole in the side of a hill and went inside because it was snowing. He slipped down a long slope, and lots of rock fell after him, and he found he could not climb up or get out again.

But almost at once he smelt goblin! and became interested, and started to explore. Not very wise; for of course goblins can't hurt him, but their caves are very dangerous.

1932

A merry christmas

Naturally he soon got quite lost, and the goblins shut off all their lights, and made queer noises and false echoes.

Goblins are to us very much what rats are to you, only worse because they are very clever; and only better because there are, in these parts, very few. We thought there were none left. Long ago we had great trouble with them – that was about 1453 I believe – but we got the help of the Gnomes, who are their greatest enemies, and cleared them out.

Anyway, there was poor old Polar Bear lost in the dark all among them, and all alone until he met Mr Cave Bear (who lives there). Cave Bear can see pretty well in the dark, and he offered to take Polar Bear to his private back-door.

So they set off together, but the goblins were very excited and angry (Polar Bear had boxed one or two flat that came and poked him in the dark, and had said some very nasty things to them all); and they enticed him away by imitating Cave Bear's voice, which of course they know very well. So Polar Bear got into a frightful dark part, all full of different passages, and he lost Cave Bear, and Cave Bear lost him.

"Light is what we need." said Cave Bear to me. So I got some of my special sparkling torches – which I sometimes use in my deepest cellars – and we set off that night.

The caves are wonderful. I knew they were there, but not how many or how big they were. Of course the goblins went off into the deepest holes and corners, and we soon found Polar Bear. He was getting quite long and thin with hunger, as he had been in the caves about a fortnight. He said, "I should soon have been able to squeeze through a goblin-crack."

Polar Bear himself was astonished when I brought light; for the most remarkable thing is that the walls of these caves are all covered with pictures, cut into the rock or painted on in red and brown and black.

Some of them are very good (mostly of animals), and some are queer and some bad; and there are many strange marks, signs and scribbles, some of which have a nasty look, and I am sure have something to do with black magic.

Cave Bear says these caves belong to him, and have belonged to him or his family since the days of his great-great-great-great-great-great-great-great-great (multiplied by ten) grandfather; and the bears first had the idea of decorating the walls, and used to scratch pictures on them on soft parts – it was useful for sharpening the claws.

Then Men came along – imagine it! Cave Bear says there were lots about at one time, long ago, when the North Pole was somewhere else. (That was long before my time, and I have never heard old Grandfather Yule mention it even, so I don't know if he is talking nonsense or not).

Many of the pictures were done by these cave-men – the best ones, especially the big ones (almost life-size) of animals, some of which have since disappeared: there are dragons and quite a lot of mammoths. Men also put some of the black marks and pictures there; but the goblins have scribbled all over the place. They can't draw well and anyway they like nasty queer shapes best.

North Polar Bear got quite excited when he saw all these things. He said: "These cave-people could draw better than you, Daddy Noel; and wouldn't your young friends just like to see some really good pictures (especially some properly drawn bears) for a change!"

Rather rude, I thought, if only a joke; as I take a lot of trouble over my Christmas pictures: some of them take quite a minute to do; and though I only send them to special friends, I have a good many in different places. So just to show him (and to please you) I have copied a whole page from the wall of the chief central cave, and I send you a copy.

It is not, perhaps, quite as well drawn as the originals (which are very, very much larger) – except the goblin parts, which are easy. They are the only parts the Polar Bear can do at all. He says he likes them best, but that is only because he can copy them.

The goblin pictures must be very old, because the goblin fighters are sitting on <u>drasils</u>: a very queer sort of dwarf 'dachshund' horse creature they used to use, but they have died out long ago. I believe the Red Gnomes finished them off, somewhere about Edward the Fourth's time.

The animal drawings are magnificent. The hairy rhinoceros looks wicked. There is also a nasty look in the mammoth's eyes. Also the ox, stag, bear, and cave-bear (portrait of Mr Cave Bear's seventy-first ancestor, he says), and some other kind of polarish but not quite polar bear. North Polar Bear would like to believe it is a portrait of one of his ancestors! Just under the bears is the best a goblin can do at drawing reindeer!!!

You have been so good in writing to me (and such beautiful letters too), that I have tried to draw you some specially nice pictures this year. At the top of my 'Christmas card' is a picture, imaginary, but more or less as it really is, of me arriving over Oxford. Your house is just about where the three little black points stick up out of the shadows at the right. I am coming from the north, and note, NOT with 12 pair of deer, as you will see in some books. I usually use 7 pair (14 is such a nice number), and at Christmas, especially if I am hurried, I add my 2 special white ones in front.

Next comes a picture of me and Cave Bear and North Polar Bear exploring the Caves – I will tell you more about that in a minute. The last picture hasn't happened yet. It soon will. On St Stephen's Day, when all the rush is over, I am going to have a rowdy party: the Cave Bear's grandchildren (they are exactly like live teddy-bears), Snowbabies, some children of the Red Gnomes, and of course Polar Cubs, including Paksu and Valkotukka, will be there.

I'm wearing a pair of new green trousers. They were a present from my green brother, but I only wear them at home. Goblins anyway dislike green, so I found them useful.

You see, when I rescued Polar Bear, we hadn't finished the adventures. At the beginning of last week we went into the cellars to get up the stuff for England. I said to Polar Bear, "Somebody has been disarranging things here!"

"Paksu and Valkotukka, I expect," he said. But it wasn't. Next day things were much worse, especially among the railway things, lots of which seemed to be missing. I ought to have guessed, and Polar Bear anyway, ought to have mentioned his guess to me.

Bless you all!

Last Saturday we went down and found nearly everything had disappeared out of the main cellar! Imagine my state of mind! Nothing hardly to send to anybody, and too little time to get or make enough new stuff.

North Polar Bear said, "I smell goblin strong." Of course, it was obvious: – they love mechanical toys (though they quickly smash them, and want more and more and more); and practically all the Hornby things had gone! Eventually we found a large hole (but not big enough for us), leading to a tunnel, behind some packing-cases in the West Cellar.

As you will expect we rushed off to find Cave Bear, and we went back to the caves. We soon understood the queer noises. It was plain the goblins long ago had burrowed a tunnel from the caves to my old home (which was not so far from the end of their hills), and had stolen a good many things.

We found some things more than a hundred years old, even a few parcels still addressed to your great-grand-people! But they had been very clever, and not too greedy, and I had not found out.

Ever since I moved they must have been busy burrowing all the way to my Cliff, boring, banging and blasting (as quietly as they could). At last they had reached my new cellars, and the sight of the Hornby things was too much for them: they took all they could.

I daresay they were also still angry with the Polar Bear. Also they thought we couldn't get at them. But I sent my patent green luminous smoke down the tunnel, and Polar Bear blew and blew it with our enormous kitchen bellows. They simply shrieked and rushed out the other (cave) end.

But there were Red Gnomes there. I had specially sent for them – a few of the real old families are still in Norway. They captured hundreds of goblins, and chased many more out into the snow (which they hate). We made them show us where they had hidden things, or bring them all back again, and by Monday we had got practically everything back. The Gnomes are still dealing with the goblins, and promise there won't be one left by New Year – but I am not so sure: they will crop up again in a century or so, I expect.

We have had a rush; but dear old Cave Bear and his sons and the Gnome-ladies helped; so that we are now very well forward and all packed. I hope there is not the faintest smell of goblin about any of your things. They have all been well aired. There are still a few railway things missing, but I hope you will have what you want. I am not able to carry quite as much toy-cargo as usual this year, as I am taking a good deal of food and clothes (useful stuff): there are far too many people in your land, and others, who are hungry and cold this winter.

I am glad that with you the weather is warmish. It is not warm here. We have had tremendous icy winds and terrific snow-storms, and my old house is quite buried. But I am feeling very well, better than ever, and though my hand wobbles with a pen, partly because I don't like writing as much as drawing (which I learned first), I don't think it is so wobbly this year.

The Polar Bear got your father's scribble to-day, and was very puzzled by it. I told him it looked like old lecture-notes, and he laughed. He says he thinks Oxford is quite a mad place if people lecture such stuff: "but I don't suppose anybody listens to it." The drawings pleased him better. He said: "At any rate those boys' father tried to draw bears – though they aren't good. Of course it is all nonsense, but I will answer it."

So he made up an alphabet from the marks in the caves. He says it is much nicer than the ordinary letters, or than Runes, or Polar letters, and suits his paw better. He writes them with the tail of his pen-holder! He has sent a short letter to you in this alphabet – to wish you a very Merry Christmas and lots of fun in the New Year and good luck at School. As you are all so clever now (he says) what with Latin and French and Greek you will easily read it and see that Polar Bear sends much love.

I am not so sure. (Anyway I dare say he would send you a copy of his alphabet if you wrote and asked. By the way he writes it in columns from top to bottom, not across: don't tell him I gave away his secret).

This is one of my very longest letters. It has been an exciting time. I hope you will like hearing about it. I send you all my love: John, Michael, Christopher, and Priscilla: also Mummy and Daddy and Auntie and all the people in your house. I dare say John will feel he has got to give up stockings now and give way to the many new children that have arrived since he first began to hang his up; but Father Christmas will not forget him. Bless you all.

Your loving, Nicholas Christmas.

To:
The Tolkiens
20 Northmoor Road
Oxford
ENGLAND

84

1933

Another Christmas!

Near North Pole
December 2nd 1933

Dear People,

Very cold here at last. Business has really begun, and we are
working hard. I have had a good many letters from you. Thank
you. I have made notes of what you want so far, but I expect I
shall hear more from you yet – I am rather short of messengers
– the goblins have – but I haven't time to tell you about our
excitements now. I hope I shall find time to send a letter later.

Give John my love when you see him. I send love to all of you,
and a kiss for Priscilla – tell her my beard is quite nice and soft,
as I have never shaved.

Three weeks to Christmas Eve!

Yours, Father Nicholas Christmas

**Cheer up, chaps (Also chaplet, if that's the feminine).
The fun's beginning!**

Yours, Polar Bear

Cliff House, near the North Pole
December 21st 1933

My dears

Another Christmas! and I almost thought at one time (in November) that there would not be one this year. There would be the 25th of December, of course, but nothing from your old great-great-etc. grandfather at the North Pole.

Goblins. The worst attack we have had for centuries. They have been fearfully wild and angry ever since we took all their stolen toys off them last year and dosed them with green smoke. You remember the Red Gnomes promised to clear all of them out. There was not one to be found in any hole or cave by New Year's day. But I said they would crop up again – in a century or so.

They have not waited so long! They must have gathered their nasty friends from mountains all over the world, and been busy all the summer while we were at our sleepiest. This time we had very little warning.

Soon after All Saints' Day, Polar Bear got very restless. He now says he smelt nasty smells – but as usual he did not say anything: he says he did not want to trouble me. He really is a nice old thing, and this time he absolutely saved Christmas. He took to sleeping in the kitchen with his nose towards the cellar-door, opening on the main-stairway down into my big stores.

One night, just about Christopher's birthday, I woke up suddenly. There was squeaking and spluttering in the room and a nasty smell – in my own best green and purple room that I had just had done up most beautifully. I caught sight of a wicked little face at the window. Then I really was upset, for my window is high up above the cliff, and that meant there were bat-riding goblins about – which we haven't seen since the goblin-war in 1453, that I told you about.

I was only just quite awake, when a terrific din began far downstairs – in the store-cellars. It would take too long to describe, so I have tried to draw a picture of what I saw when I got down – after treading on a goblin on the mat.

Only ther was more like 1000 goblins than 15.

(But you could hardly expect me to draw 1000). Polar Bear was squeezing, squashing, trampling, boxing and kicking goblins skyhigh, and roaring like a zoo, and the goblins were yelling like engine whistles. He was splendid.

Say no more – I enjoyed it immensely!

Well, it is a long story. The trouble lasted for over a fortnight, and it began to look as if I should never be able to get my sleigh out this year. The goblins had *send lots of love.*

set part of the stores on fire and captured several gnomes, who sleep down there on guard, before Polar Bear and some more gnomes came in – and killed 100 before I arrived.

Even when we had put the fire out and cleared the cellars and house (I can't think what they were doing in my room, unless they were trying to set fire to my bed) the trouble went on. The ground was black with goblins under the moon when we looked out, and they had broken up my stables and gone off with the reindeer.

I had to blow my golden trumpet (which I have not done for many years) to summon all my friends. There were several battles – every night they used to attack and set fire in the stores – before we got the upper hand, and I am afraid quite a lot of my dear elves got hurt.

Fortunately we have not lost much except my best string, (gold and silver) and packing papers and holly-boxes. I am very short of these: and I have been very short of messengers. Lots of my people are still away (I hope they will come back safe) chasing the goblins out of my land, those that are left alive.

They have rescued all my reindeer. We are quite happy and settled again now, and feel much safer. It really will be centuries before we get another goblin-trouble. Thanks to Polar Bear and the gnomes, there can't be very many left at all.

And Father Christmas. I wish I could draw or had time to try – you have no idea what the old man can doo! Litening and fierworks and thunder of guns!

Polar Bear certainly has been busy helping, and double help – but he has mixed up some of the girls' things with the boys' in his hurry. We hope we have got all sorted out – but if you hear of anyone getting a doll when they wanted an engine, you will know why. Actually Polar Bear tells me I am wrong – we did lose a lot of railway stuff – goblins always go for that – and what we got back was damaged and will have to be repainted. It will be a busy summer next year.

Now, a merry Christmas to you all once again. I hope you will all have a very happy time; and will find that I have taken notice of your letters and sent you what you wanted. I don't think my pictures are very good this year – though I took quite a time over them (at least two minutes). Polar Bear says, "I don't see that a lot of stars and pictures of goblins in your bedroom are so frightfully merry." Still I hope you won't mind. It is rather good of Polar Bear kicking, really. Anyway I send lots of love.

Yours ever and annually
Father Nicholas Christmas.

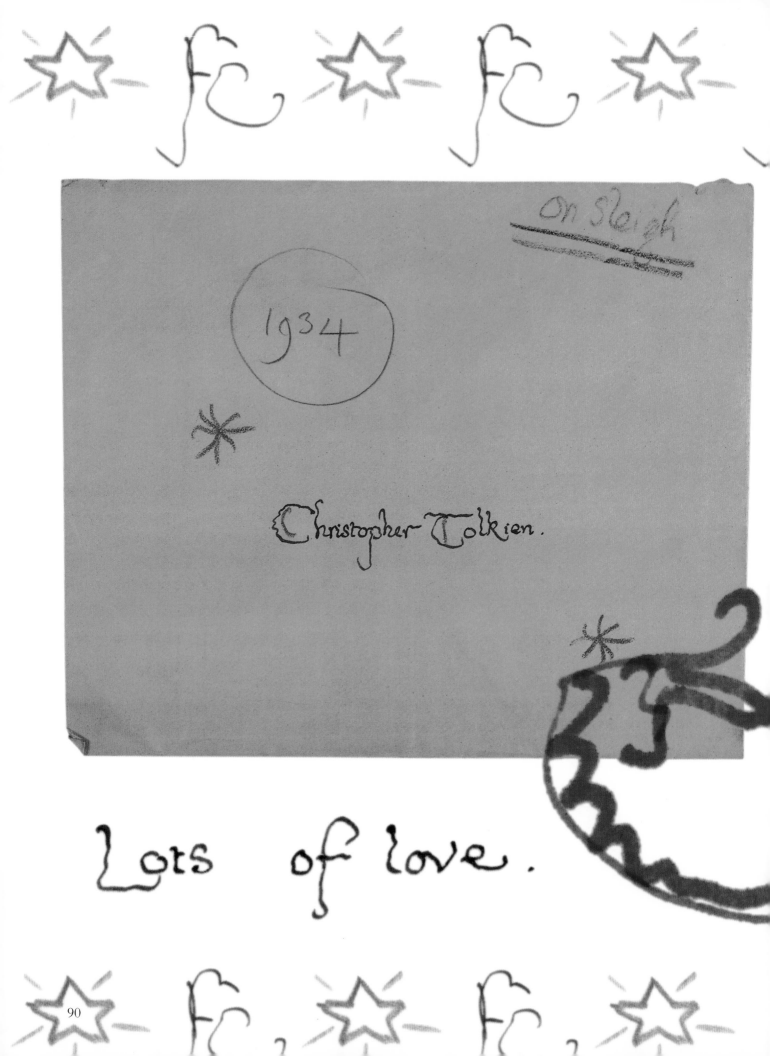

On sleigh

1934

Christopher Tolkien.

Lots of love.

1934

91

1934

!! To messenger: Deliver at once and don't stop on the way!!

At once   Urgent   Express!

My dear Christopher

Thank you! I am awake – and have been a long while. But my post office does not really open ever until Michaelmas. I shall not be sending my messengers out regularly this year until about October 15th. There is a good deal to do up here. Your telegram – that is why I have sent an express reply – and letter and Priscilla's were found quite by accident: not by a messenger but by Bellman (I don't know how he got that name because he never rings any; he is my chimney inspector and always begins work as soon as the first fires are lit).

Very much love to you and Priscilla. (The Polar Bear, if you remember him, is still fast asleep, and quite thin after so much fasting. He will soon cure that. I shall tickle his ribs and wake him up soon; and then he will eat several months' breakfast all in one).

More love, your loving Father Christmas

Cliff House, North Pole
Christmas Eve. 1934

My dear Christopher

Thank you very much for your many letters. I have not had time this year to write you so long a letter as 1932 and 1933, but nothing at all exciting has happened. I hope I have pleased you with the things I am bringing and that they are near enough to your lists.

Very little news: after the frightful business of last year there has not been even a smell of goblin for 200 miles round. But, as I said it would, it took us far into the summer to repair all the damage, and we lost a lot of sleep and rest.

When November came round we did not feel like getting to work, and we were rather slow and so have been rushed at the end. Also it has been unusually warm for the North Pole, and the Polar Bear still keeps on yawning.

Paksu and Valkotukka have been here a long while. They have grown a good deal – but still get up to frightful mischief in between times of trying to help. This year they stole my paints and painted scrawls on the white walls of the cellars; ate all the mincemeat out of the pies made ready for Christmas; and only yesterday went and unpacked half the parcels to find railway things to play with!

They don't get on well with the Cave cubs, somehow; several of these have arrived today and are staying here a few nights with old Cave Brown Cave, who is their uncle, granduncle, grandfather, great granduncle, etc. Paksu is always kicking them because they squeak and grunt so funnily: Polar Bear has to box him often – and a 'box' from Polar Bear is no joke.

As there are no Goblins about, and as there is no wind, and so far much less snow than usual, we are going to have a great boxing-day party ourselves – out of doors. I shall ask 100 elves and red gnomes, lots of polar cubs, cave-cubs, and snowbabies, and of course, Paksu and Valkotukka, and Polar Bear and Cave Bear and his nephews (etc.) will be there.

We have brought a tree all the way from Norway and planted it in a pool of ice. My picture gives you no idea of its size, or of the loveliness of its magic lights of different colours. We tried them yesterday evening to see if they were all right. If you see a bright glow in the North you will know what it is!

Behind the tree are snowplants, and piled masses of snow made into ornamental shapes – they are purple and black because of darkness and shadow. There is also a special edging to the ice-pool – and it is made of real coloured icing. Paksu and Valkotukka are already nibbling at it, though they should not – till the party.

Polar Bear started to draw this to help me, as I was busy, but he dropped such blots – enormous ones. I had to come to the rescue. Not very good this year. Never mind: perhaps better next year.

I hope you will like your presents and be very happy.

Your loving
Father Christmas.

PS I really can't remember exactly in what year I was born. I doubt if anyone knows. I am always changing my own mind about it. Anyway it was 1934 years ago or jolly nearly that.
Bless you! FC
PPS Give my love to Mick and John.

Polar Bear LOVE BISY THANKS

Christmas 1934

N 36 P

Master C & Miss P. Tolkien
20 Northmoor Road
Oxford
ENGLAND

My Dear Children

North Pole

1935

December 24 1935
North Pole

My dear Children

Here we are again. Christmas seems to come round pretty soon again: always much the same and always different. No ink this year and no water, so no painted pictures; also very cold hands, so very wobbly writing.

Last year it was very warm, but this year it is frightfully cold – snow, snow, snow, and ice. We have been simply buried, messengers have got lost and found themselves in Nova Scotia, if you know where that is, instead of in Scotland; and PB, if you know who that is, could not get home.

This is a picture of my house about a week ago before we got the reindeer sheds dug out. We had to make a tunnel to the front door. There are only three windows upstairs shining

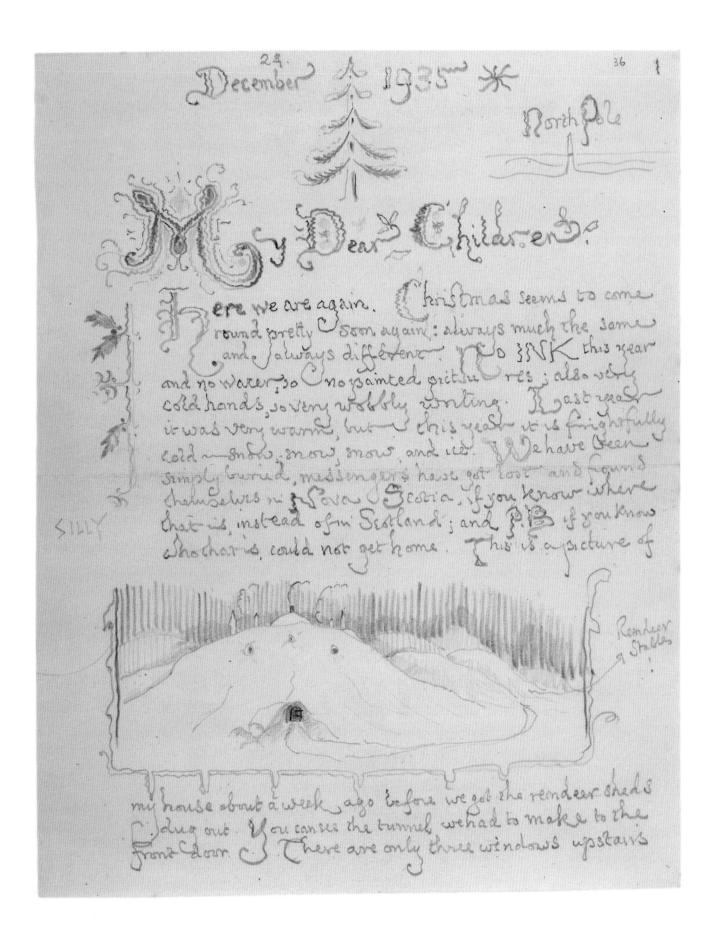

December 1935

North Pole

My Dear Children:

Here we are again. Christmas seems to come round pretty soon again: always much the same and always different. No INK this year and no water, so no painted pictures; also very cold hands, so very wobbly writing. Last year it was very warm, but this year it is frightfully cold — snow, snow, snow, and ice. We have been simply buried, messengers have got lost and found themselves in Nova Scotia, if you know where that is, instead of in Scotland; and P.B. if you know who that is, could not get home. This is a picture of

SILLY

Reindeer Stables

my house about a week ago before we got the reindeer sheds dug out. You can see the tunnel we had to make to the front door. There are only three windows upstairs

99

1935

through holes – and there is steam where the snow is melting off the dome and roof.

This is a view from my bedroom window. Of course, snow coming down is not blue – but blue is cold: You can understand why your letters were slow in going. I hope I got them all, and anyway that the right things arrive for you.

Poor old PB, if you know who I mean, had to go away soon after the snow began last month. There was some trouble in his family, and Paksu and Valkotukka were ill. He is very good at doctoring anybody but himself.

But it is a dreadfully long way over the ice and snow – to North Greenland I believe. And when he got there he could not get back. So I have been rather held up, especially as the Reindeer stables and the outdoor store sheds are snowed over.

I have had to have a lot of Red Elves to help me. They are very nice and great fun; but although they are very quick they don't get on fast. For they turn everything into a game. Even digging snow. And they will play with shining through holes — but you can see steam where the snow is melting off the dome and roofs. This a view from my bedroom window. Of course snow

coming down is not blue — but blue it is cold! You can understand why your letters were slow in going & those I got them all, and anyway that the right things arrive for you. Poor old PB, it you who I mean, had to go away soon after the snow began last month. There was some trouble in his family, and Paksu & Valkotukka were ill. He — very good at doctoring anybody but himself. But it it's a dreadfully long way over the ice and snow to North Greenland, I believe. And when he got there he could not get back. So I have been rather held up, especially as the Reindeerstables and the outdoor store sheds are snowed over. I have had to have a

SILLY AGAIN

lot of Red Elves to help me. They are very nice & great fun; but although they are very quick they don't get on fast. For they turn everything into a game. Even digging snow. And they will play with the toys they are supposed to be packing.

PB, if you remember him, did not get back until Friday December 13th – so that proved a lucky day for me after all!

(HEAR HEAR!)

Even he had to wear a sheepskin coat and red gloves for his paws. And he had got a hood on and red gloves. He thinks he looks rather like Rye St Anthony. But of course he does not very much. Anyway he carries things in his hood – he brought home his sponge and soap in it!

He says that we have not seen the last of the goblins – in spite of the battles in 1933. They won't dare to come into my land yet; but for some reason they are breeding again and multiplying all over the world. Quite a nasty outbreak. But there are not so many in England, he says. I expect I shall have trouble with them soon.

I have given my elves some new magic sparkler spears that will scare them out of their wits. It is now December 24th and they have not appeared this year – and practically everything is packed up and ready. I shall be starting soon the toys they are supposed to be packing.

P.B., if you remember him, did not get back until Sunday December the 13th — so that proved a lucky day for me (HEAR HEAR!) after all. Even he had to wear a sheepskin coat & red gloves for his paws. And he had odd gloves. He rather like But of course a hood on and red trunks he looked Rt St Anthony he does not very

much. Any way he carries things in his hood — he brought home his sponge and soap in it!

He says that we have not seen the last of the goblins — inspite of the battles in 1933. They won't dare to come into my land yet; but for some reason they are breeding again and multiplying all over the world — quite a nasty outbreak! But there are not so many in England, he says. I expect I shall have trouble with them soon. I have given my elves

Some new magic sparkler spears that will scare them out of their wits. It is now December 24 and they have not appeared this year — and practically everything is packed up and ready. I shall be starting soon

103

I send you all – John and Michael and Christopher and Priscilla – my love and good wishes this Christmas: tons of good wishes. Pass on a few if you don't want them all! Polar Bear (in case you don't know what PB is) sends love to you – and to the Bingos and to Orange Teddy and to Jubilee. (O yes I learn lots of news even in Snowy weather). My messengers will be about until the New Year if you want to write and tell me everything was all right.

I hope you enjoy the pantomime

Your loving
Father Christmas

PS Paksu and Valkotukka are well again. Only mumps. They will be at my big party on St Stephen's Day with other polar cubs, cave cubs, snowbabies, elves, and all the rest.

1935

I send you all — John & Michael & Christopher & Priscilla — my love and good wishes this Xmas: tons of good wishes. Pass on a fewif you don't want them all!

STUPID JOKE ✳ PB

Polar Bear (in case you don't know what P.B is) sends love to you — and to the Bingos and to Orange Teddy and to Jubilee (O yes I learn lots of news even in Snowy weather) My messengers will be about until the New Year if you want to write and tell me everything was all right. I hope you enjoy the

PANTOMIME

Your loving

Father Christmas

P.S. P. & V are well again. Only shrimps. They will beat my big party on St Stephen's Day with other polar cubs, cave cubs, snowbabies, elves, and all the rest.

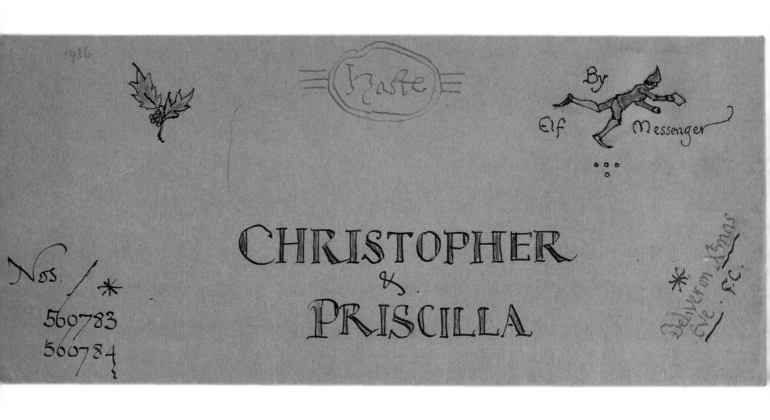

1936

Haste

By Elf Messenger

CHRISTOPHER
&
PRISCILLA

Noss. /*
560783
560784

Deliver on Xmas
Eve. FC.

I send very much love to you all.

North Pole

1936

My dear Children

Cliff House
North Pole
Wednesday Dec. 23rd 1936

My dear Children

I am sorry I cannot send you a long letter to thank you for yours, but I am sending you a picture which will explain a good deal. It is a good thing your changed lists arrived before these awful events, or I could not have done anything about it. I do hope you will like what I am bringing and will forgive any mistakes, and I hope nothing will still be wet! I am still so shaky and upset, I am getting one of my elves to write a bit more about things.

I send very much love to you all.

Father Christmas says you will want to hear some news. Polar Bear has been quite good – or had been – though he has been rather tired. So has Father Christmas; I think the Christmas business is getting rather too much for them.

So a lot of us, red and green elves, have gone to live permanently at Cliff House, and be trained in the packing business. It was Polar Bear's idea. He also invented the number system, so that every child that Father Christmas deals with has a number and we elves learn them all by heart, and all the addresses. That saves a lot of writing.

Cliff House.
North Pole
"
Wednesday Dec. 23rd
1936

My dear Children

I am sorry I cannot send you a
long letter to thank you for yours, but
I am sending you a picture which will explain
a good deal. It is a good thing your
changed lists arrived before these awful
events, or I could not have done anything
about it. I do hope you will like what I am
bringing and will forgive any mistakes, & I
hope nothing will still be wet! I am
still so shaky and upset. I am getting one of
my elves to write a bit more about things.
I send very much love to you all.

father C. says you will want to hear some news. PB has been quite
good — or had been — though he has been rather tired. So has F.C. I think
the Christmas business is getting rather too much for them. So a lot of us,
red and green elves, have gone to live permanently at Cliff House, and be
trained in the packing business. It was P.B's idea. He also invented the
number system, so that every child that F.C. deals with has a number
and we elves learn them all by heart, and all the addresses. that saves

So many children have the same name that every packet used to have the address as well. Polar Bear said: "I am going to have a record year and help Father Christmas to get so forward we can have some fun ourselves on Christmas day."

We all worked hard, and you will be surprised to hear that every single parcel was packed and numbered by Saturday (December 19th). Then Polar Bear said "I am tired out: I am going to have a hot bath, and go to bed early!"

Well you can guess what happened. Father Christmas was taking a last look round in the English Delivery Room about 10 o'clock when water poured through the ceiling and swamped everything: it was soon 6 inches deep on the floor. Polar Bear had simply got into the bath with both taps running and gone fast asleep with one hind paw on the overflow. He had been asleep two hours when we woke him.

Father Christmas was really angry. But Polar Bear only said: "I did have a jolly dream. I dreamt I was diving off a melting iceberg and chasing seals."

He said later when he saw the damage: "Well there is one thing: those children at Northpole Road, Oxford (he always says that) may lose some of their presents, but they will have a letter worth hearing this year. They can see a joke, even if none of you can!"

That made Father Christmas angrier, and Polar Bear said: "Well, draw a picture of it and ask them if it is funny or not." So Father Christmas has. But he has begun to think it funny (although very annoying) himself, now we have cleared up the mess, and got the English presents repacked again. Just in time. We are all rather tired, so please excuse scrawly writing.

Yours, Ilbereth, Secretary to Father Christmas

Very sorry. Been bizy. Can't find that alphabet. Will look after Christmas and post it. Yours, Polar Bear.

.P.B.

Yrs F.C

Best
Wishes
for.
1
9
3
7

from
F·C
&
P·B
?

Xmas 1
9
3
6
∴
F·C·

TIMES

560,783
560,784

A·Merry·Christmas

42

I HAVE FOUND IT. I SEND YOU
A COPY. YOU NEEDNT FILL IN
BLACK PARTS IF YOU DONT
WANT TO. IT TAKES RATHER
LONG TO RITE BUT I THINK
IT IS RATHER CLEVER.
     STILL BIZY. F.C. SEZ I CANT
HAVE A BATH TILL NEXT YEAR.
LOVE TOU YO BOTH BICAUSE
YOU SEE JOKES
                    P.B.

     I GOT INTO HOT WATER
DIDNT I?   HA! HA!   P.B.

I have found it. I send you a copy. You needn't fill in black parts if you don't want to. It takes rather long to rite but I think it is rather clever.

Still bizy. Father Christmas sez I can't have a bath till next year.

Love tou yo both bicause you see jokes

Polar Bear

I got into hot water didn't I? Ha! Ha!

GOBLIN ALPHABET

43

A   AI

L   OR

     ALL OR AW

B

M

C   CH

N

O   OA   OU OR OW   OI

D

P   PH

E   EA

QU

   EI

R   OR

      NG

   EU OR EW

S   SH

T   TH

DOUBLE SIGN

     SO

F

G   OR

     = EE

   GH

H

W   WH

     = AND

U

V

I

X

J

Y

K

Z

CK

113

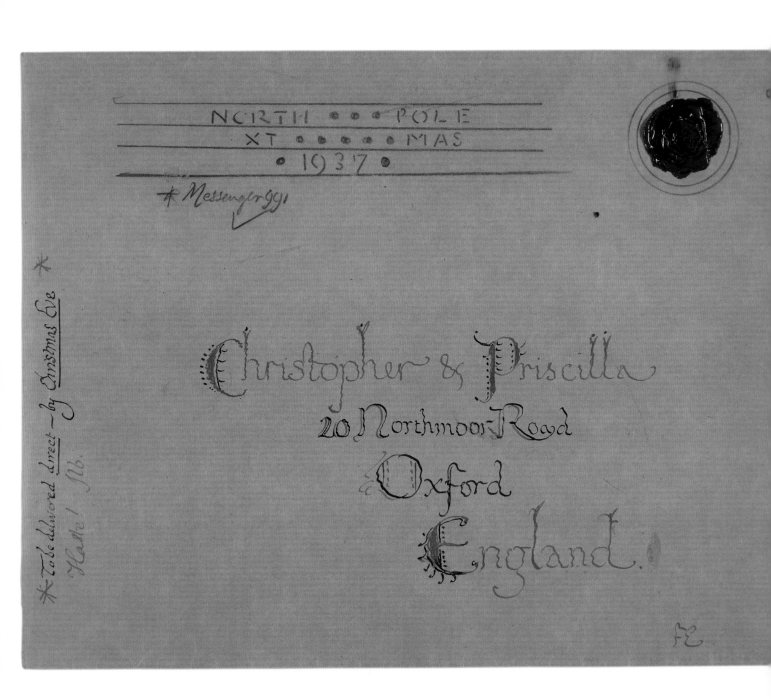

NORTH • • • POLE
XT • • • • • • MAS
• 1937 •

✳ Messenger 991

✳ To be delivered direct — by Christmas Eve.
Haste! Nb.

Christopher & Priscilla
20 Northmoor Road
Oxford
England.

FC

1937

My dear Christopher and Priscilla,

Cliff House, North Pole
Christmas 1937

My dear Christopher and Priscilla, and other old friends in Oxford: here we are again!

Of course I am always here (when not travelling), but you know what I mean. Christmas again. I believe it is 17 years since I started to write to you. I wonder if you have still got all my letters? I have not been able to keep quite all yours, but I have got some from every year.

We had quite a fright this year. No letters came from you. Then one day early in December I sent a messenger who used to go to Oxford a lot but had not been there for a long while, and he said: "Their house is empty and everything is sold." I was afraid something had happened, or that you had all gone to school in some other town, and your father and mother had moved. Of course, I know now; the messenger had been to your old house next door! He complained that all the windows were shut and the chimneys all blocked up.

I was very glad indeed to get Priscilla's first letter, and your two nice letters, and useful lists and hints, since Christopher came back. I quite understand that School makes it difficult for you to write like you used. And of course I have new children coming on my lists each year so that I don't get less busy.

Tell your father I am sorry about his eyes and throat: I once had my eyes very bad from snow-blindness, which comes from looking at sunlit snow. But it got better. I hope Priscilla and

your Mother and everyone else will be well on Dec. 25. I am afraid I have not had any time to draw you a picture this year. You see I strained my hand moving heavy boxes in the cellars in November, and could not start my letters until later than usual, and my hand still gets tired quickly. But Ilbereth – one of the cleverest Elves who I took on as a secretary not long ago – is becoming very good.

He can write several alphabets now – Arctic, Latin (that is ordinary European like you use), Greek, Russian, Runes, and of course Elvish. His writing is a bit thin and slanting – he has a very slender hand – and his drawing is a bit scratchy, I think. He won't use paints – he says he is a secretary and so only uses ink (and pencil). He is going to finish this letter for me, as I have to do some others.

So I will now send you lots of love, and I do hope that I have chosen the best things out of your suggestion lists. I was going to send 'Hobbits' – I am sending away loads (mostly second editions) which I sent for only a few days ago – but I thought you would have lots, so I am sending another Oxford Fairy Story.

Lots and Lots of Love, Father Christmas

Dear Children:

I am Ilbereth. I have written to you before. I am finishing for Father Christmas. Shall I tell you about my pictures? Polar Bear and Valkotukka and Paksu are always lazy after Christmas, or rather after the St Stephen's Day party. Father Christmas is ringing for breakfast in vain. Another day when Polar Bear, as usual, was late

not true!

Paksu threw a bath-sponge full of icy water on his face. Polar Bear chased him all round the house and round the garden and then forgave him, because he had not caught Paksu, but had found a huge appetite.

We had terrible weather at the end of winter and actually had rain. We could not go out for days. I have drawn Polar Bear and his nephews when they did venture out. Paksu and Valkotukka have never gone away. They like it so much that they have begged to stay.

It was much too warm at the North Pole this year. A large lake formed at the bottom of the Cliff, and left the North Pole standing on an island. I have drawn a view looking South, so the Cliff is on the other side. It was about mid-summer. The North Polar Bear, his nephews and lots of polar cubs used to come and bathe. Also seals. North Polar Bear took to trying to paddle a boat or canoe, but he fell in so often that the seals thought he liked it, and used to get under the boat and tip it up. That made him annoyed.

The sport did not last long as the water froze again early in August. Then we began to begin to think of this Christmas. In my picture Father Christmas is dividing up the lists and giving me my special lot – you are in it.

North Polar Bear of course always pretends to be managing everything: that's why he is pointing, but I am really listening to Father Christmas and I am saluting him not North Polar Bear.

Rude little errand boy.

We had a glorious bonfire and fireworks to celebrate the Coming of Winter and the beginning of real 'Preparations'. The Snow came down very thick in November and the elves and snowboys had several tobogganing half-holidays. The polar cubs were not good at it. They fell off, and most of them took to rolling or sliding down just on themselves. Today – but this is the best bit, I had just finished my picture, or I might have drawn it differently.

And better!

Polar Bear was being allowed to decorate a big tree in the garden, all by himself and a ladder. Suddenly are heard terrible growly squeaky noises. We rushed out to find Polar Bear hanging on the tree himself!

"You are not a decoration," said Father Christmas.
"Anyway, I am alight," he shouted.

He was. We threw a bucket of water over him. Which spoilt a lot of the decorations, but saved his fur. The silly old thing had rested the ladder against a branch (instead of the trunk of the tree). Then he thought, "I will just light the candles to see if they are working," although he was told not to. So he climbed to the tip of the ladder with a taper. Just then the branch cracked, the ladder slipped on the snow, and Polar Bear fell into the tree and caught on some wire; and his fur got caught on fire.

Poor joke.

Luckily he was rather damp or he might have fizzled. I wonder if roast Polar is good to eat?

Not as good as well spanked and fried elf.

The last picture is imaginary and not very good. But I hope it will come true. It will if Polar Bear behaves. I hope you can read my writing. I try to write like dear old Father Christmas (without the trembles), but I cannot do so well. I can write Elvish better:

That is some – but Father Christmas says I write even that too spidery and you would never read it.

Love Ilbereth.

A big hug and lots of love. Enormous thanks for letters. I don't get many, though I work so harrd. I am practising new writing with lovely thick pen. Quicker than Arctick. I invented it.

Ilbereth is cheky. How are the Bingos? A merry Christmas. North Polar Bear

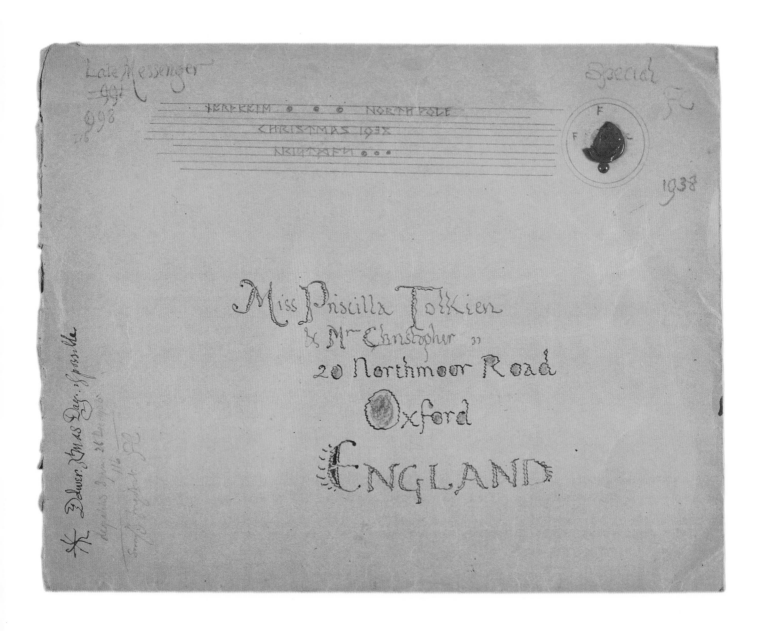

Late Messenger
991
998

Special

~~IMPRRIM~~ ∘ ∘ ∘ NORTH POLE
CHRISTMAS 193X
NRISTARIN ∘ ∘ ∘

F
F

1938

Miss Priscilla Tolkien
& Mr Christopher "
20 Northmoor Road
Oxford
ENGLAND

Deliver Xmas Day. if possible

Cliff House, North Pole
Christmas 1938

My dear Priscilla and all others at your house

Here we are again! Bless me, I believe I said that before – but after all you don't want Christmas to be different each year, do you?

I am frightfully sorry that I haven't had the time to draw any big picture this year, and Ilbereth (my secretary) has not done one either; but we are all sending you some rhymes instead. Some of my other children seem to like rhymes, so perhaps you will.

We have all been very sorry to hear about Christopher. I hope he is better and will have a jolly Christmas. I only heard lately when my messengers and letter collectors came back from Oxford. Tell him to cheer up – and although he is now growing up and leaving stockings behind, I shall bring a few things along this year. Among them is a small astronomy book which gives a few hints on the use of telescopes – thank you for telling me he had got one. Dear me! My hand is shaky – I hope you can read some of this?

I loved your long letter, with all the amusing pictures. Give my love to your Bingos and all the other sixty (or more!), especially Raggles and Preddley and Tinker and Tailor and Jubilee and Snowball. I hope you will go on writing to me for a long while yet.

Very much love to you – and lots for Chris – from

Father Christmas

SETTING OUT.

Again this year, my dear Priscilla,
when you're asleep upon your pillow;

**Bad rhyme!
That's beaten you!**

beside your bed old Father Christmas

[The English language has no rhyme
to Father Christmas: that's why I'm
not very good at making verses.
But what I find a good deal worse is
that girls' and boys' names won't rhyme either
(and bother! either won't rhyme neither).
So please forgive me, dear Priscilla,
if I pretend you rhyme with pillow!]

She won't.

As I was saying -

beside your bed old Father Christmas
(afraid that any creak or hiss must

How's that?

Out!

wake you up) will in a twinkling
fill up your stocking, *(I've an inkling
that it belongs, in fact, to pater –
but never mind!)* At twelve, or later,
he will arrive – and hopes once more
that he has chosen from his store

I did it.

the things you want. You're half past nine;

She is not a clock!

but still I hope you'll drop a line
for some years yet, and won't forget
old Father Christmas and his Pet,
the North Polar Bear (and Polar Cubs
as fat as little butter-tubs),
and snowboys and Elves – in fact the whole
of my household up near the Pole.

Blots by P and V

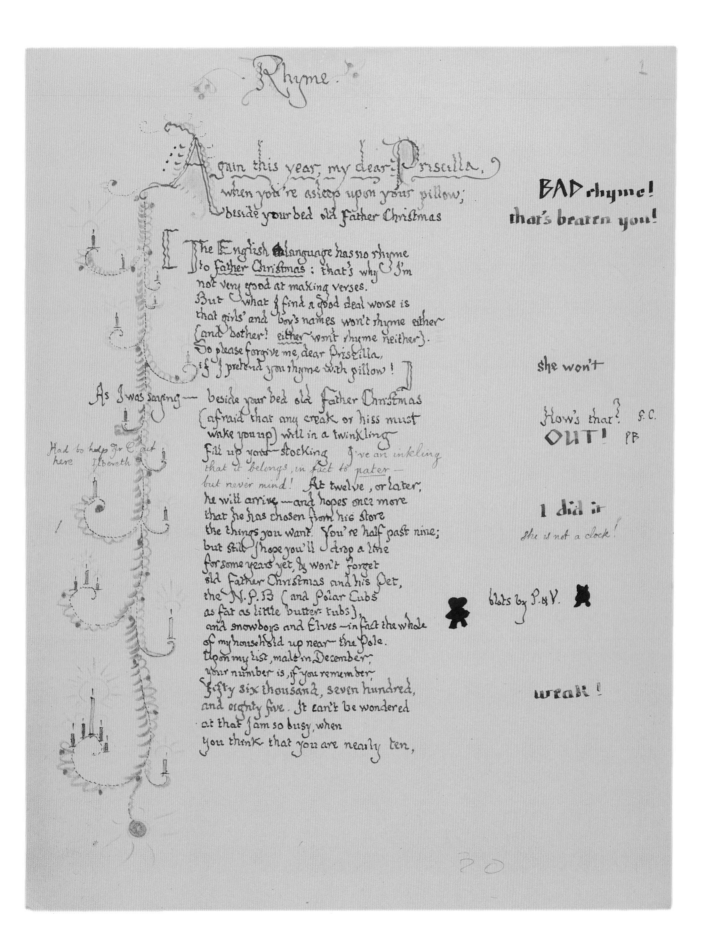

Rhyme.

Again this year, my dear Priscilla,
when you're asleep upon your pillow;
beside your bed old Father Christmas

BAD rhyme!
that's beaten you!

[The English alanguage has no rhyme
to Father Christmas: that's why I'm
not very good at making verses.
But what I find a good deal worse is
that girls' and boy's names won't rhyme either
(and bother! either won't rhyme neither).
So please forgive me, dear Priscilla,
if I pretend you rhyme with pillow!]

she won't

As I was saying — beside your bed old Father Christmas
(afraid that any creak or hiss must
wake you up) will in a twinkling
fill up your stocking I've an inkling
that it belongs, in fact to pater —
but never mind! At twelve, or later,
he will arrive — and hopes once more
that he has chosen from his store
the things you want. You're half past nine;
but still I hope you'll drop a line
for some years yet, & won't forget
old Father Christmas and his Pet,
the N. P. B. (and Polar Cubs
as fat as little butter tubs),
and snowboys and Elves — in fact the whole
of my household up near the Pole.
Upon my list, made in December,
your number is, if you remember,
fifty six thousand, seven hundred,
and eighty five. It can't be wondered
at that I am so busy, when
you think that you are nearly ten,

How's that? F. C.
OUT! PB

I did it
she is not a clock!

blots by P. & V.

weak!

Had to help Fr. C. out
here Ilbereth

1

Upon my list, made in December,
your number is, if you remember,
fifty six thousand, seven hundred,
and eighty five. It can't be wondered

Weak!

at that I am so busy, when
you think that you are nearly ten,
and in that time my list has grown
by quite ten thousand girls alone,
even when I've subtracted all
the houses where I no longer call!

You all will wonder what's the news;
if all has gone well, and if not who's
to blame; and whether Polar Bear
has earned a mark good, bad, or fair,
for his behaviour since last winter.
Well – first he trod upon a splinter,

**Just rhiming nonsens: it
was a nail – rusty, too**

and went on crutches in November;
and then one cold day in December
he burnt his nose and singed his paws
upon the Kitchen grate, because
without the help of tongs he tried
to roast hot chestnuts. "Wow!" he cried,

I never did!

and used a pound of butter (best)
to cure the burns. He would not rest,

I was not given a chance.

but on the twenty-third he went
and climbed up on the roof. He meant
to clear the snow away that choked
his chimney up – of course he poked
his legs right through the tiles and snow

in tons fell on his bed below.
He has broken saucers, cups, and plates;
and eaten lots of chocolates;
he's dropped large boxes on my toes,
and trodden tin-soldiers flat in rows;

**You need not
believe all this!**

You need!

he's over-wound engines and broken springs,
and mixed up different children's things;
he's thumbed new books and burst balloons
and scribbled lots of smudgy Runes
on my best paper, and wiped his feet
on scarves and hankies folded neat –
And yet he has been, on the whole,
a very kind and willing soul.
He's fetched and carried, counted, packed
and for a week has never slacked:

here hear!

I wish you wouldn't scribble
on my nice rhyme!

he's climbed the cellar-stairs at least
five thousand times – the Dear Old Beast!

Paksu sends love and Valkotukka –
They are still with me, and they don't look a
year older, but they're just a bit
more wise, and have a pinch more wit.

The GOBLINS, you'll be glad to hear,
have not been seen at all this year,
not near the Pole. But I am told,
they're moving south, and getting bold,
and coming back to many lands,
and making with their wicked hands
new mines and caves. But do not fear!
They'll hide away, when I appear.

129

Christmas Day

Now Christmas Day has come round again –
and poor North Polar Bear has got a bad pain!
They say he's swallowed a couple of pounds
of nuts without cracking the shells! It sounds
a Polarish sort of thing to do –
but that isn't all, between me and you:
he's eaten a ton of various goods
and recklessly mixed all his favourite foods,
honey with ham and turkey with treacle,
and pickles with milk. I think that a week'll
be needed to put the old bear on his feet.
And I mustn't forget his particular treat:
plum pudding with sausages and turkish delight
covered with cream and devoured at a bite!
And after this dish he stood on his head –
it's rather a wonder the poor fellow's not dead!

Absolute ROT:
I have not got
a pain in my pot.

Rude fellow!

I do not eat
turkey or meat:
I stick to the sweet.
Which is why
(as all know) I
am so sweet myself,
you thinuous elf!
Goodby!

He means fatuous

No I don't, you're not fat,
but thin and silly.

You know my friends too well to think
(although they're rather rude with ink)
that there are really quarrels here!
We've had a very jolly year
(except for Polar Bear's rusty nail);
but now this rhyme must catch the Mail –
a special messenger must go,

in spite of thickly falling snow,
or else this won't get down to you
on Christmas day. It's half past two!
We've quite a ton of crackers still
to pull, and glasses still to fill!
Our love to you on this Noel –
and till the next one, fare you well!

Father Christmas
Polar Bear
Ilbereth
Paksu and Valkotukka

131

1939

Priscilla Tolkien

1939

Cliff House, NORTH POLE
December 24th 1939

My dear Priscilla

I am glad you managed to send me two letters although you have been rather busy working. I hope your Bingo family will have a jolly Christmas, and behave themselves. Tell Billy – is not that the father's name? – not to be so cross. They are not to quarrel over the crackers I am sending.

I am very busy and things are very difficult this year owing to this horrible war. Many of my messengers have never come back. I haven't been able to do you a very nice picture this year. It is supposed to show me carrying things down our new path to the sleigh-sheds. Paksu is in front with a torch looking most frightfully pleased with himself (as usual). There is just a glimpse (quite enough) of Polar Bear strolling along behind. He is of course carrying nothing.

There have been no adventures here, and nothing funny has happened – and that is because Polar Bear has done hardly anything to "help", as he calls it, this year.

ROT!

I don't think he has been lazier than usual, but he has been not at all well. He ate some fish that disagreed with him last November and was afraid he might have to go to hospital in Greenland. But after living only on warm water for a fortnight he suddenly threw the glass and jug out of the window and decided to get better.

He drew the trees in the picture, and I am afraid they are not very good.

Best part of it

They look more like umbrellas! Still he sends love to you and all your bears. "Why don't you have Polar Cubs instead of Bingos and Koalas?" he says.

Why not?

Give my love to Christopher and Michael and to John when you next write.

Love from Father Christmas.

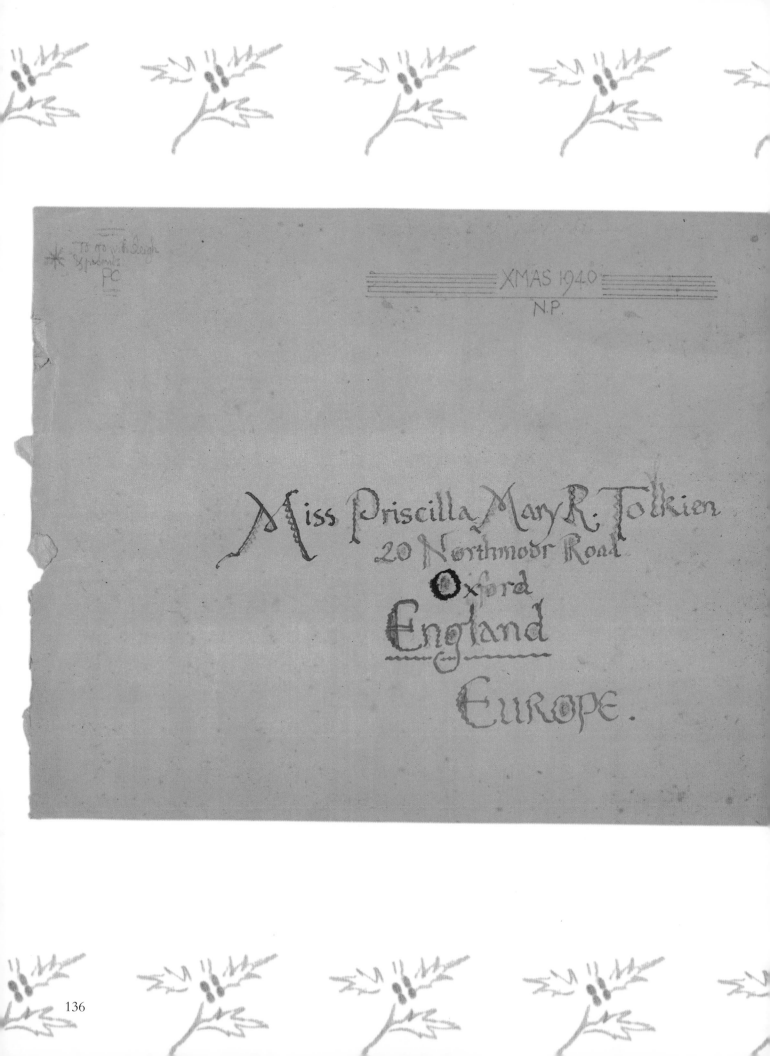

XMAS 1940
N.P.

Miss Priscilla Mary R. Tolkien
20 Northmoor Road
Oxford
England
Europe.

1940

Christmas

December 23rd 1940

Dear Priscilla

Glad to find you are back! Message came on Saturday
that your house was empty. Wos afrade you had gon
without leaving any address.

Ar having verry DIFFICULT time this year but ar doing
~~my~~ our best.

THANK YOU for explaining about your room. Father
Christmas sends love! Please excuse blots. Rather bizzy.

Yours Polar Bear

yours
P.B.

FC

love

2am. Dec. 13ʰ

FR. CHRIST
MAS. SAYS
O.K.
yrs. P.B.

⟨no⟩ don't
say all right'
FC.

Cliff House, near North Pole
Christmas Eve 1940

My Dearest Priscilla

Just a short letter to wish you a very happy Christmas. Please give my love to Christopher. We are having rather a difficult time this year. This horrible war is reducing all our stocks, and in so many countries children are living far from their homes. Polar Bear has had a very busy time trying to get our address-lists corrected. I am glad you are still at home!

I wonder what you will think of my picture. "Penguins don't live at the North Pole," you will say. I know they don't, but we have got some all the same. What you would call "evacuees", I believe (not a very nice word); except that they did not come here to escape the war, but to find it! They had heard such stories of the happenings up in the North (including a quite untrue story that Polar Bear and all the Polar Cubs had been blown up, and that I had been captured by Goblins) that they swam all the way here to see if they could help me. Nearly 50 arrived.

The picture is of Polar Bear dancing with their chiefs. They amuse us enormously: they don't really help much, but are always playing funny dancing games, and trying to imitate the walk of Polar Bear and the Cubs.

Father Christmas

VERY MUCH LOVE FROM YOUR
OLD FRIEND
. Father Christmas .

Cliff House, near (stump of) North Pole
December 22nd, 1941

My Dearest Priscilla,

I am so glad you did not forget to write to me again this year.
The number of children who keep up with me seems to be
getting smaller: I expect it is because of this horrible war, and
that when it is over things will improve again, and I shall be as
busy as ever. But at present so terribly many people have lost
their homes: or have left them; half the world seems in the
wrong place.

And even up here we have been having troubles. I don't mean
only with my stores: of course they are getting low. They were
already last year, and I have not been able to fill them up, so
that I have now to send what I can instead of what is asked for.
But worse than that has happened.

I expect you remember that some years ago we had trouble
with the Goblins; and we thought we had settled it. Well, it
broke out again this autumn, worse than it has been for
centuries. We have had several battles, and for a while my
house was besieged. In November it began to look likely that
it would be captured and all my goods, and that Christmas
Stockings would all remain empty all over the world.

Would not that have been a calamity? It has not happened –
and that is largely due to the efforts of Polar Bear –

N.B. That's mee!

but it was not until the beginning of this month that I was
able to send out any messengers! I expect the Goblins thought
that with so much war going on this was a fine chance to
recapture the North. They must have been preparing for some
years; and they made a huge new tunnel which had an outlet
many miles away.

It was early in October that they suddenly came out in
thousands. Polar Bear says there were at least a million.,
but that is his favourite big number.

There wer at leest a hundred million.

Miss P. M. R. Tolkien
OXFORD
England.

1941.

My Dearest Priscilla

Anyway, he was still fast asleep at the time, and I was rather drowsy myself; the weather was rather warm for the time of the year and Christmas seemed far away. There were only one or two elves about the place; and of course Paksu and Valkotukka (also fast asleep). The Penguins had all gone away in the spring.

Luckily Goblins cannot help yelling and beating on drums when they mean to fight; so we all woke up in time, and got the gates and doors barred and the windows shuttered. Polar Bear got on the roof and fired rockets into the Goblin hosts as they poured up the long reindeer-drive; but that did not stop them for long. We were soon surrounded.

I have not time to tell you all the story. I had to blow three blasts on the great Horn (Windbeam). It hangs over the fireplace in the hall, and if I have not told you about it before it is because I have not had to blow it for over 4 hundred years: its sound carries as far as the North Wind blows. All the same it was three whole days before help came: snowboys, polar bears, and hundreds and hundreds of elves.

They came up behind the Goblins: and Polar Bear (really awake this time) rushed out with a blazing branch off the fire in each paw. He must have killed dozens of Goblins (he says a million).

But there was a big battle down in the plain near the North Pole in November, in which the Goblins brought hundreds of new companies out of their tunnels. We were driven back to the Cliff, and it was not until Polar Bear and a party of his younger relatives crept out by night, and blew up the entrance to the new tunnels with nearly 100lbs of gunpowder that we got the better of them – for the present.

But bang went all the stuff for making fireworks and crackers (the cracking part) for some years. The North Pole cracked and fell over (for the second time), and we have not yet had time to mend it. Polar Bear is rather a hero (I hope he does not think so himself)

I DO!

But of course he is a very MAGICAL animal really,

N. B.

and Goblins can't do much to him, when he is awake and angry. I have seen their arrows bouncing off him and breaking.

Well, that will give you some idea of events, and you will understand why I have not had time to draw a picture this year – rather a pity, because there have been such exciting things to draw – and why I have not been able to collect the usual things for you, or even the very few that you asked for.

I am told that nearly all the Alison Uttley books have been burnt, and I could not find one of 'Moldy Warp'. I must try and get one for next time. I am sending you a few other books, which I hope you will like. There is not a great deal else, but I send you very much love.

I like to hear about your Bear Bingo, but really I think he is too old and important to hang up stockings! But Polar Bear seems to feel that any kind of bear is a relation. And he said to me, "Leave it to me, old man (that, I am afraid is what he often calls me): I will pack a perfectly beautiful selection for his Poliness (yes, Poliness!)". So I shall try and bring the 'beautiful selection' along: what it is, I don't know!

Very much love from your old friend Father Christmas
and Polar Bear

145

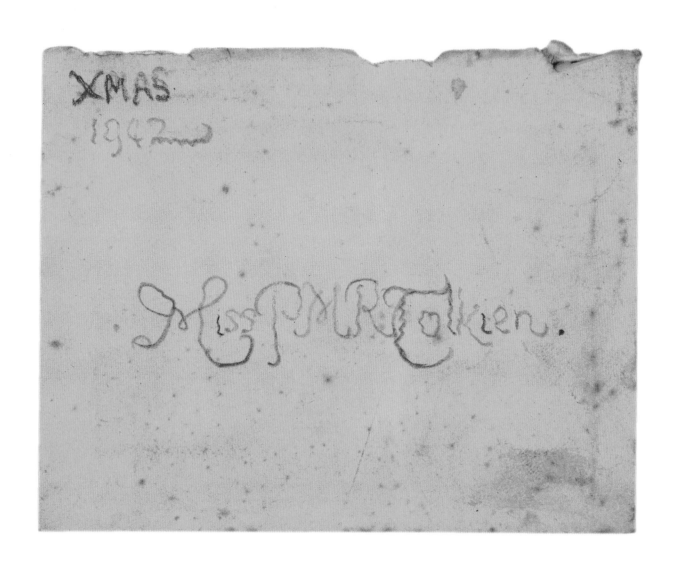

XMAS
1942

Miss P M R Tolkien.

Cliff House, North Pole
Christmas Eve 1942

My dear Priscilla,

Polar Bear tells me that he cannot find my letter from you among this year's piles. I hope he has not lost any: he is so untidy. Still I expect you have been very busy this autumn at your new school.

I have had to guess what you would like. I think I know fairly well, and luckily we are still pretty well off for books and things of that sort. But really, you know, I have never seen my stocks so low or my cellars so full of empty places (as Polar Bear says).

I am hoping that I shall be able to replenish them before long; though there is so much waste and smashing going on that it makes me rather sad, and anxious too. Deliveries too are more difficult than ever this year with damaged houses and houseless people and all the dreadful events going on in your countries. Of course it is just as peaceful and merry in my land as ever it was.

We had our snow early this year and then nice crisp frosty nights to keep it white and firm, and bright starry 'days' (no sun just now of course).

I am giving as big a party tomorrow night as ever I did, polar cubs (Paksu and Valkotukka, of course, among them) and snowboys, and elves. We are having the Tree indoors this year – in the hall at the foot of the great staircase, and I hope Polar Bear does not fall down the stairs and crash into it after it is all decorated and lit up.

I hope you will not mind my bringing this little letter along with your things tonight: I am short of messengers, as some have great trouble in finding people and have been away for days. Just now I caught Polar Bear in my pantry, and I am sure he had been to a cupboard. I do not know why.

very much love fro

Cliff House.
NORTH POLE.
CHRISTMAS 1942.

My dear Priscilla,

P.B. tells me that he cannot find any letter from you among this year's piles. I hope he has not lost any: he is so untidy. Still I expect you have been very busy this autumn at your new school. I have had to guess what you would like. I think I know fairly well, and luckily we are still pretty well off for books and things of that sort. But really, you know, I have never seen my stocks so low or my cellars so full of "empty places" (as P.B. says, although he is not an Irish bear). I am hoping that I shall be able to replenish them before long; though there is so much waste and smashing going on that it makes me rather sad and anxious too. Deliveries too are more difficult than ever this year with damaged houses and houseless people and all the dreadful events going on in your countries. Of course it is just as peaceful and merry in my land as ever it was.* We had our snow early this year and then nice crisp frosty nights to keep it white and firm, and bright starry days (no sun just now of course). I am giving as big a party tomorrow night as ever I did, polar cubs (P. & T. of course among them) and snowboys, and elves. We are having the Tree indoors this year — in the hall at the foot of the great staircase, and I hope P.B. does not fall down the stairs and crash into it after it is all decorated and lit up. I hope you will not mind my bringing this little letter along with your things tonight: I am short of messengers, as some have great trouble in finding people and have been away for days. Just now I caught P.B. in my pantry, and I am sure he had been to a cupboard. I do not know why. He has wrapped up a mysterious small parcel which he wants me to bring to you — "well not exactly to you (he said): she has got a bear too, as you ought to remember." Well my dear here is very much love from Father Christmas once more, and very good wishes for 1943 ⨏

* No battles at all this year. Quiet as quiet. I think the Goblins were really crushed this time. Windbeam is hanging over the mantlepiece and is quite dusty again, I am glad to say. But P.B. has spent lots of time this year making fresh gunpowder — just in case of trouble. He said "wouldn't that grubby P.T.O.

Father Christmas

He has wrapped up a mysterious small parcel which he wants me to bring to you – well not exactly to you (he said): "She has got a bear too, as you ought to remember."

Well my dear here is very much love from Father Christmas once more, and very good wishes for 1943.

*No battles at all this year. Quiet as quiet. I think the Goblins were really crushed this time. Windbeam is hanging over the mantelpiece and is quite dusty again, I am glad to say. But Polar Bear has spent lots of time this year making fresh gunpowder – just in case of trouble. He said, "wouldn't that grubby little Billy like being here!" I don't know what he was talking about, unless it was about your bear: does he eat gunpowder?

You'll find out about the pantry! Ha! Ha! I know wot you like. Don't let that Billy Bear eat it all!
Love from Polar Bear.

Messige to Billy Bear from Polar Bear
Sorry I could not send you a really good bomb. All our
powder has gone up in a big bang. You would have seen
wot a really good exploashion is like. If yould been there.

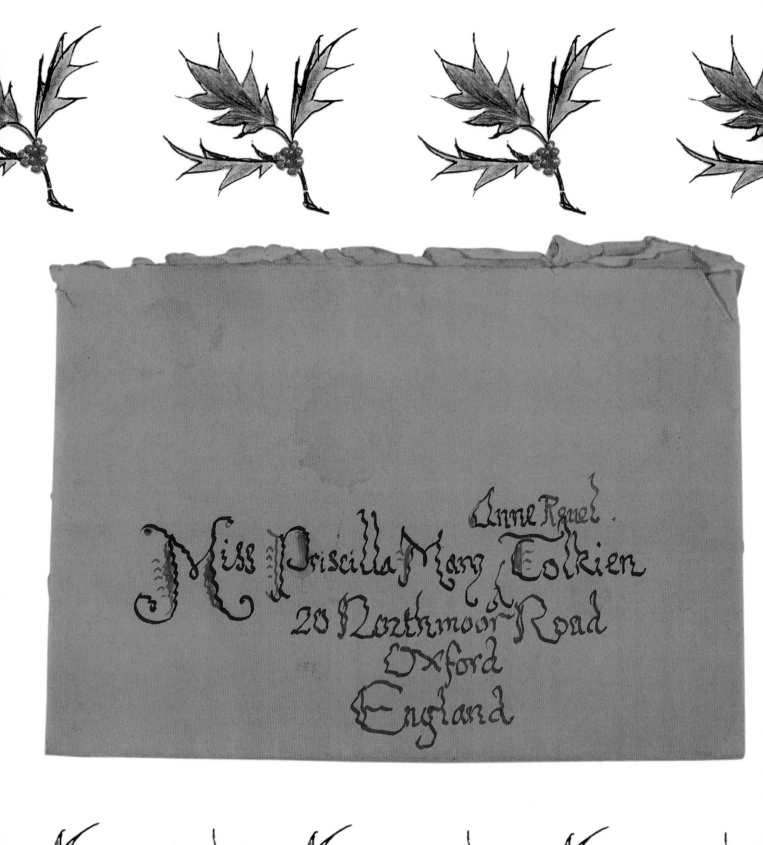

Anne Rquel.

Miss Priscilla Mary Tolkien
20 Northmoor Road
Oxford
England

1943.

'Father Christmas

My dear Priscilla

Cliff House, North Pole, Christmas 1943

My dear Priscilla

A very happy Christmas! I suppose you will be hanging up your stocking just once more: I hope so for I have still a few little things for you. After this I shall have to say "goodbye", more or less: I mean, I shall not forget you. We always keep the old numbers of our old friends, and their letters; and later on we hope to come back when they are grown up and have houses of their own and children.

My messengers tell me that people call it "grim" this year. I think they mean miserable: and so it is, I fear, in very many places where I was specially fond of going; but I am very glad to hear that you are still not really miserable. Don't be! I am still very much alive, and shall come back again soon, as merry as ever. There has been no damage in my country; and though my stocks are running rather low I hope soon to put that right.

Polar Bear – too "tired" to write himself (so he says) –

I am, reely

sends a special message to you: love and a hug! He says: do ask if she still has a bear called Silly Billy, or something like that; or is he worn out?

Give my love to the others: John and Michael and Christopher – and of course to all your pets that you used to tell me about. Polar Bear and all the Cubs are very well. They have really been very good this year and have hardly had time to get into any mischief.

I hope you will find most of the things that you wanted and I am very sorry that I have no 'Cats' Tongues' left. But I have sent nearly all the books you asked for. I hope your stocking will seem full!

Very much love from your old friend, Father Christmas.

A very happy Christmas!

Very much love

"goodbye"

WORKS BY J. R. R. TOLKIEN

The Hobbit
The Lord of the Rings
Leaf by Niggle
On Fairy Stories
The Homecoming of Beorhtnoth
Farmer Giles of Ham
The Adventures of Tom Bombadil
Smith of Wootton Major
The Road Goes Ever On (with Donald Swann)

Works published posthumously

The Silmarillion
The Father Christmas Letters
Sir Gawain, Pearl and Sir Orfeo
Pictures by J.R.R. Tolkien
Unfinished Tales
The Letters of J.R.R. Tolkien
Mr Bliss
The Monsters and the Critics
Finn and Hengest
Roverandom

THE HISTORY OF MIDDLE-EARTH
by Christopher Tolkien

I The Book of Lost Tales, Part One
II The Book of Lost Tales, Part Two
III The Lays of Beleriand
IV The Shaping of Middle-earth
V The Lost Road and Other Writings
VI The Return of the Shadow
VII The Treason of Isengard
VIII The War of the Ring
IX Sauron Defeated
X Morgoth's Ring
XI The War of the Jewels
XII The Peoples of Middle-earth